MOVING ON

MOVING ON

MICHAEL FOOT

Copyright © 2018 Michael Foot

The moral right of the author has been asserted.

Apart from any fair dealing for the purposes of research or private study,
or criticism or review, as permitted under the Copyright, Designs and Patents
Act 1988, this publication may only be reproduced, stored or transmitted, in
any form or by any means, with the prior permission in writing of the
publishers, or in the case of reprographic reproduction in accordance with
the terms of licences issued by the Copyright Licensing Agency. Enquiries
concerning reproduction outside those terms should be sent to the publishers.

This is a work of fiction. Names, characters, businesses, places, events
and incidents are either the products of the author's imagination
or used in a fictitious manner. Any resemblance to actual persons,
living or dead, or actual events is purely coincidental.

Matador
9 Priory Business Park,
Wistow Road, Kibworth Beauchamp,
Leicestershire. LE8 0RX
Tel: 0116 279 2299
Email: books@troubador.co.uk
Web: www.troubador.co.uk/matador
Twitter: @matadorbooks

ISBN 978 1788038 690

British Library Cataloguing in Publication Data.
A catalogue record for this book is available from the British Library.

Printed and bound in the UK by 4edge limited
Typeset in 11 pt Minion Pro by Troubador Publishing Ltd, Leicester, UK

Matador is an imprint of Troubador Publishing Ltd

To our 3 children, Anthony, Helen and Joanna,
who have made my world a much better place.

1

A QUIET DAY FOR AN HONEST HACK

Harry felt good as he walked up Whitehall. His first meeting was at 11a.m. and only 20 minutes' walk from the apartment, so he had a good enough excuse not to go into the office first. That in turn had allowed more time in bed with Carol; and, almost as satisfying, the chance to drink a pot of coffee unhurriedly over the morning papers.

He knew that the lull in his diary schedule would be temporary. His editor would accept another day or two of 'background for the next story'; his last filing had been good enough to ensure that, with gratifying attention to it from the competition. But that was, now literally, old news and anyway he was bored with it. Inshallah; something new would appear; but Harry knew it would be better for him to go and find it than wait for it to come to him. Even with his reputation – which often encouraged people to bring him leads – it was rare indeed for a story to reach his door without it needing a lot more work. Investigative journalism – though not a term widely used these days – was, he knew only too well, largely a combination of sweat, luck and timing.

His call at the Ministry this morning would probably not help much, though his contact had been strangely insistent that Harry came. The bureaucrat involved, Simon Pike, had helped with a story once or twice but only after Harry had done the legwork first. Harry could never recall him providing something genuinely new. But Simon did know a lot of people – in part thanks to the persistent efforts of his wife to push his career. And a well-placed Interior Ministry official willing to help at all was not so common-place as to be safe to ignore.

The thought of Tara, Simon's wife, brought a quick moment of distaste. If Harry was honest (which he usually was with himself even if he didn't always act on the upshot of his musing), his feelings about Tara were ambivalent. On the plus side, she dressed well, looked good and could be good company. Against that, Tara clearly didn't rate Harry to be worth much of an effort. If they talked at a party, her eyes would roam the room looking for a more interesting, influential mark to engage. And, while Harry was used to such treatment by a proportion of his contacts, the way Tara did it always got under his skin; he resented both her and the fact that she annoyed him.

Harry had never been sure exactly what Tara had seen in Simon. She had picked him up when they were both at Cambridge; and – even nearing 40 – Simon could still be an engaging and intelligent man. Certainly, Tara would have known from the start that she could always get Simon to do what she wanted. But Harry wondered sometimes if Tara really had understood early on that Simon would never hit any great heights. With Simon, Tara's ambitions would always fall back to Earth; or, as now, circle at a strictly limited altitude in the little political world she so enjoyed.

A sudden full-on image of Tara made Harry stumble slightly as he went up the steps of the Ministry. Yes, perhaps he was just a little cowed by her.

The woman who escorted him up to Simon's Third Floor office spoke only in monosyllables and few of those. From past experience, Harry expected Simon's secretary to usher him into a little waiting room, until she judged that Harry had waited long enough to be sufficiently reminded of his strictly limited standing. She would then allow an audience to begin. But, on this occasion, the secretary – Jill he thought her name was – actually smiled at him and waved him straight into Simon's office. *"I know he's expecting you, Mr Woods; go in. The Minister will be with you shortly."*

Strange, thought Harry. Why would a Minister – even one of the 7 or 8 relatively junior ones who made up the Parliamentary cast at the Ministry – come to Simon's room? Or to see him?

Stranger still, there was Simon on the other side of the door, obviously awaiting him. His face showed a clear tension, only just overlaid by the good natured, slightly quizzical, exterior that Simon typically showed to the world. *"Good to see you Harry and on time too. Gives me a minute to brief you… before he comes"*

"What is going on?" said Harry. *"Which Minister am I to be blessed by and why? Surely your lords and masters haven't taken offence at anything I've written lately? Or does one of your Ministers want to chuck it in and start writing half-truths for my paper rather than telling them in the Commons?"*

"Nothing like that; and I do wish you'd be a bit more respectful. Believe me, it's no easy job being a Minister these days, any more than it is being one of their supposedly expert

advisers. Anyway that's what I wanted to say before he gets here so you won't cock it up. It's" and his voice shrank to a conspiratorial whisper *"it's not one of **my** Ministers, it's Hetman. And he specially asked me to get you here today. I hope you feel duly honoured. The official story is that he is here to see the Home Secretary and he's dropping a present off with me for Tara's birthday. He and Tara have been friends for years."*

Harry's gut instinct told him that something was wrong. He had never seen Hetman except at a crowded press conference. A strong (many said the strongest) rising star in the PDP Government. Already Secretary-General of the PDP, although still under 40. Currently, a Minister without Portfolio, whose main job seemed to be saving the Prime Minister's skin twice a week, taking no prisoners in the process. A man who looked and sounded good on a screen with an impeccable life story –orphaned at 12 and then making good through his own efforts. Just the kind of man Harry would normally go some way to avoid; and who, he would have thought, would have as little to say to Harry as Harry would have to say to him.

"I'm honoured but a little bewildered, Simon. I hope you haven't been promising my paper's support for the Election or anything else I can't deliver. I may be a successful hack and I may have a long rein when it comes to what I do. But I'm just a hack. And, as you know, I draw the line at explicitly political stories."

Simon backed into his seat and took refuge behind his ample and expensive-looking desk. *"Oh no. You can definitely do what he wants. Tara is sure of it – it was her idea you know. This man's going all the way, Harry; make no mistake. I'm giving you the chance to jump on the express while it's still moving at walking speed."*

2

A SIMPLE REQUEST

To ask is no sin and to be refused is no calamity
– Russian proverb

There was perhaps a minute's silence and then Simon's secretary reappeared in the doorway. *"The Minister"* she said, holding the door wide.

Simon and Harry rose as one. But anything Simon was going to say by way of welcome was swept aside by Hetman's immediate control of the room. *"No formality gentlemen please. This isn't an official visit. I am just dropping in on the husband of an old friend. And here.."* Hetman extended an arm in Harry's direction – *"is the bonus of meeting someone I've long hoped to bump into."* The secretary withdrew, shutting the door behind her, having duly heard the 'official story'.

Simon's office was big enough to accommodate a small sofa and 2 chairs. Hetman sank into the sofa, motioning Simon and Harry to take the 2 matching chairs. He looked at Harry. *"So this is Harry Woods, the man who has made and broken more public careers than any other British journalist writing today. And you could pass for an ordinary Joe on the street by the look of you."*

Harry protested gently. *"I think that's one of my strengths, Minister. I've never imagined myself as anything special or as a deus ex machina determining careers – for good or ill. I just write stories about the things I see in public and business life. Sometimes that throws up heroes, sometimes villains; but very often I'm just writing about people who find themselves out of their depth and who did what they genuinely thought was the best. My story often just starts the fairground ride. As you may know, I'm very careful over what I publish. Double check, triple check so that my readers know they aren't being fed the usual biased half-truths. I have no agenda, no party favours to curry. I just write about what affects ordinary people and I bring out into the open what never should have been hidden from them in the first place."*

"Of course" Hetman responded, holding his palms out towards Harry as though seeking to placate him, though Harry had in no way been aggressive. *"What little I know about the 'real' you is more than enough to tell me I'd be wasting my time if I were here to try and bribe you... or threaten you. It's exactly your independence and public standing that I need to have. So let me get straight to the point and see if I can interest you in what I have in mind."*

There was a short pause. Simon shifted in his chair and it dawned on Harry that, for Simon Pike, the next few minutes were somehow critical. Simon had been the conduit by which Hetman had got to Harry. Simon's face was drawn, his mouth slightly open and his forehead was visibly damp with sweat that hadn't been there before. Maybe the outcome of the next few minutes, Harry realised, might determine the class or even the existence of Simon's own ticket on the Hetman Express.

Hetman seemed to make a decision and launched

himself, leaning forward on the sofa and looking hard at Harry. *"You know as well as anyone that the next Election is 6 months away. And you know, as well as anyone, that there isn't the slightest doubt we will get another thumping majority, even if we don't roll out many sweeteners in advance for the electorate. I sometimes detect in your writing that you hanker for the old days of Government and Opposition. But the fact is that the PDP has sewn up modern politics. And, for now at least, that is how it's going to be.*

So, for the foreseeable future, the PDP is destined to be both the Government and His Majesty's loyal Opposition – or at least different factions within the PDP will be. The real debate about strategy, about where the country's going, needs to take place within the PDP – it's not going to happen anywhere else.

I freely admit that this debate currently isn't all it should be. Far too many complacent MPs, happy to hang on to what they've got. Other people within the PDP like me want to move forward, air innovative policies, get them debated, get established in the public eye as the coming political generation.

*That's where you come in. I'm willing to tell you **now** what my group within the PDP is going to roll out in a month's time as what we see as **the** key issue of the next few years. I'll give you the chance to consider it, do some investigative work and then write up your views as the debate unfolds. I can get you unprecedented access – here and in Europe – so that you can write authoritatively about it. And, in the process you'll have had a great time."*

Harry waited a few seconds. *"And if I don't come down on your side of whatever this 'great debate' is?"* *"That's a risk I'm prepared to take"* replied Hetman. *"The mere fact*

7

that you write about the subject will help to launch the debate. If you don't fully subscribe to our views, you may come up with ideas that we can incorporate, to improve our plans. And I think, anyway, you'll be very hard put to argue that we haven't put the spotlight onto a huge problem, which future Governments will have no choice but to tackle somehow. Now, perhaps Simon you could pop out and get us something for lunch from the local sandwich bar –I'll take ham and cheese on rye please – while I explain to Harry just what I have in mind."

3

A SIMPLE IDEA

"There are three kinds of lies; lies, damned lies and statistics."

– Benjamin Disraeli.

When they were alone, Hetman focused his attention firmly on Harry. The latter had a mental picture of Hetman as a rather large reptile, not the leonine image he thought Hetman might have pictured for himself. The Minister began without further ado.

"How old are you, Harry – 53 isn't it?" Harry nodded. *"So, maybe another 10-12 years working and then a well-deserved retirement?"* Again, Harry nodded. *"Well, I apologise for throwing statistics at you. But do you realise by the time you retire, Harry, that the number of the sick and the elderly will have actually come to exceed the number of people still working? And do you also realise that, by the time you die – maybe 20 years later – on present trends there will be around 1.2 non-workers for every worker? The ageing of the population has been going on for several decades now. But it's reaching crisis proportions. Just the same is true in other countries.*

Now, Harry, you no doubt are one of those who may have planned ahead and actually have something to live off to supplement your Government handouts in retirement. But for most people that just isn't true – many of them will end their working days in debt, lonely and frightened. And, whenever these people are ill, the cost of that also falls back on the State.

The state of Government finances means that the Government of the day will always be looking to pull back whatever it can of the support rug the old have got used to. Not an attractive idea for us in Government or for those actually going into retirement. And every time there is another medical breakthrough – on cancer or whatever – the economics gets worse; the treatment will cost money, it will prolong essentially non-productive lives. Do you know the great unspoken fear in the Economics Ministry? That some idiot goes and discovers a way to stop and reverse cell deterioration – at which point every old person will clamour for the treatment and for every last day of active life they can wring out of the system. The whole government financial jigsaw – which now is held together mainly by hope and the unwillingness to look ahead – will collapse.

To get across just what a seismic shift has been going on, let me tell you that around 1850, if you survived to the age of 10, your life expectancy was 70. By 1970 that figure had risen to 72. By the early 2000s we were talking about average life expectancy for men of about 80 years, for women over 85. In 1850 there were 2.5 workers for every child and elderly person; soon it's going to be 0.8."

Hetman let this raft of statistics sink gently in. Harry said nothing. Hetman continued. *"The problem won't go away. Indeed, even the average worker has started to realise that the burden of taxes can only rise further; and that every time he or she finds a way of improving productivity, the net result is often a pitiful reward for those actually making the changes. Ordinary working people have real wages that are little or no higher than they were 30 years ago. It can't go on or there will be a revolt by those in work – not the kind of thing the PDP, or any Government, would want. And that fact – together with some critical ideas of how to break the logjam – is what we plan to launch debate on in a month's time."*

Harry spoke at last. *"Good luck to you. The old will just want the problem buried until they can be too. As for your average worker, he or she doesn't think much about next year let alone 20 or 30 years ahead. And, presumably any ideas you have for changing the situation significantly are going to require some pretty unpalatable medicine being swallowed by workers or by the old. As I say, good luck.""That's exactly why we need someone like you deeply involved in getting a proper debate under way"* replied Hetman. *"We have some great ideas for a New Deal for the elderly. We can promise them a better life while at the same time leaving some money on the table for those who actually produce our wealth.*

But who is readily going to believe us? We need someone with credibility and proven integrity. We need that person to investigate what currently happens, consider whether it can indeed continue; and comment on our 'solutions'. In short, we need Harry Woods to get involved, understand the issues properly and write them up for his public. The time and elbow-room to do that, with your editor's blessing – once we have had a preliminary word with him to smooth the way – is exactly what we are offering you. With no strings attached." On this note, the door opened and Simon returned, with a small tray of sandwiches and a paper carrier bag of what turned out to be fruit and juices. *"Going well?* asked Simon. Hetman looked at him impassively. *"Yes I think so. I was just about to invite Harry to dine at my club soon, so that he can hear more."*

4

WHAT COULD BE EASIER?

"Oldness has come; old age has descended. Feebleness has arrived; dotage is here anew. The heart sleeps wearily every day....God is become evil. All taste is gone. What old age does to men is evil in every respect."
– Extract from a lament of an ancient Egyptian. From George Minois 'History of old age: from Antiquity to the Renaissance.'

So, just 2 evenings later, Harry found himself enjoying an excellent Chateauneuf du Pape and a tenderloin steak at Hetman's club. Harry had not been hard to persuade. He rarely ate well enough to turn down a good meal lightly. And it occurred to him that to be seen out with Hetman could do his standing with many of his normal contacts no harm at all. This was the kind of thing that got noticed even if it didn't get into the gossip columns.

Hetman played the good host and it was not until dessert that he brought the conversation round to the supposed theme. *"Now, this is a world-wide problem not just here in England. Indeed, I'll start with an illustration from Japan. In Tokyo, the number of people over 65 has risen from 2.7 million in 2010 to over 4 million now. One-*

third of all Tokyo inhabitants are now over 65, about one in 6 is over 75. Add to that the hundreds of thousands of carers and what do you have? A situation where every worker pays for almost one old person, which will happen in Japan by 2065. Already two-thirds of the local government budget there goes on social care, mostly for the old.

And it can only get worse. Fertility rates world-wide in developed countries are now below replacement levels. Almost every year we hear of another miracle medical or pharmaceutical discovery that extends life expectancy yet further. Where will it be in 10 years time? What will we do if we can effectively abolish cancer, prevent dementia and – far more important – reverse the ageing process?

This way lies a revolt by the working class as they realise what they have let themselves in for. National output will fall and there will be an impossible budget situation for any government. The old would clamour for every life-extending innovation to be financed for their benefit on the NHS. That can't be financed. So, in the long run the old probably won't do very well anyway.

*The main difference then is that people are living **much** longer and there aren't throngs of young people around them to hide them and carry the costs. I was reading the other day that some of our forebears found some clever ways to deal with the problem. Did you know, it's thought that our ancestors established that the right place for older people – once they couldn't hunt or work – was round the outside of the camp fire or at the edge of the cave? That way, not only did the heat get to those who most needed it and had the power to take what they wanted. But any marauding predator would be likely to get a stomach full of granny, not one of the tribe's hunters or young. Straight thinking, if a bit abrasive for our tastes.*

And as for the old themselves, there have of course been lots of cultures where the old were actually encouraged to take their own lives, to avoid being a burden. Even the saintly Thomas More thought that an early planned death for the elderly was a great idea – my memory is that he favoured the application of large amounts of opium."

At this point, a large raspberry fell off Hetman's spoon and into the excellent fruit coulis that they had both chosen for dessert. That helped Harry to snap out of his apparent reverie. *"And so what is your group advocating then to deal with this? Euthanasia?"*

"Hardly" replied Hetman. *"We have to offer something that will attract older people to want it, and younger people to support it because they can see financial and other benefits; if possible, we also need to produce a solution that helps Government politically as well as financially. And that is what I think we have got. Before I get to that, though, what do you know about the current 'Moving On' programme?"*

A light dawned for Harry. *"Ah, you're thinking of some ramped up version of the current programme. Well, all I know about that is that it's about 5 years old and, in a low key way, offers modest tax and other incentives to older people to agree to relocate and sever connections with their family and friends here. It's hardly a pressing concern for me at my age, though I did have on older work colleague who used it."*

Hetman smiled as though Harry had just correctly completed a school test. *"Yes, Harry. It's actually about 7 years old and, as a result of it, we've now got about 100,000 people of 70 or over residing – in some comfort I may say – in the South-West. There they get specialist health support that it just wouldn't be worth providing unless it can serve a lot of elderly people together. Their basic needs are fully catered for, they get spending money. They can have a society of like-minded people, with carers and medical support thrown in. They do a bit of work if they're up to it and want to, grow a lot of their own vegetables for enjoyment; generally I'm told they have a high old time.*

Their relatives inherit, on a tax-friendly basis, the individual's assets the day he or she moves over. The individual has to agree that all links will be severed, though the system does allow for the odd (postal) message to be sent by those left, for example to tell of a new grandchild or a marriage. For those left behind, it's very much as though the older person has died suddenly. But any family or friends know they're actually alive and well. They will never know when the individual does actually die; but they can say goodbye to them in the Moving On ceremony; and then know their relatives are getting a standard of care that could never be afforded if they stayed in their existing community. All at a net saving of about 30% compared with what the cost of their ageing would otherwise have been; and a better life for the old person.

Hetman paused briefly. *"We've learned a lot about how the scheme should really work and are ready to scale it up hugely and quickly with even greater savings. There are millions of old people, most of them poor, neglected and constantly fighting to get the medical attention they need. For most of them, the transition would be a kindness – a 'win' for both old and young. The old need encouragement to embrace the unknown; they need to know how it could improve their lives. Younger people need to understand how they will benefit, even if it means losing granny a few years earlier than they might have wanted. I don't think grandpa will be missed too much. As I said, before, we need a Harry*

Woods to take a good hard look up and down and tell them how he thinks it could be."

Harry in turn looked hard at Hetman. *"So, let me put this in my own words. What you want is for me to get to understand the dynamics and economics of what being old in England really means today. You want me to visit these model towns of the future you already have. By the sound of what you said when we first met, you also want me to draw some international comparisons, at least within Europe. You'd like that largely done and dusted within the month, so you can launch your debate. And – this goes without saying for me but I'll spell it out for you – this is all to be done with **me** determining the agenda, going where **I** want, speaking to whom I want. And you'll fix it with my editor up front."*

Hetman smiled thinly. *"If you work as fast and with as much focus as you talk, a month should be more than enough. Simon can be your contact. Think about it overnight, contact him and then – if you're happy – start on the detailed planning with him on Monday. I happen to know that you don't have much on the work front just now."*

5

PLANNING BEGINS

A journey of 1,000 miles begins with the first step.
  – **Lao Tsu in the *Tao Te Ching*, chapter 64.**

Harry had long established a system for helping him reach any important decision. The day after Hetman had dined him so well, Harry found a quiet hour back in his flat and laid a single piece of paper out on his desk. He drew 2 columns on the sheet, headed – not very innovatively – 'Plus' and 'Minus' and allowed himself 15 minutes to think about each.

At the end of 15 minutes, the 'plus' column – as to why Harry should take this on – had some respectable entries:a) **saves money**. Hetman had effectively promised Harry 4 weeks work with all expenses paid. Harry wasn't so well off that a free month's pay from his paper would come amiss; b) **involves travel**. Like most people, since the fracturing of British links with the world after BREXIT and the traumas of the plague in the 20s, Harry had done remarkably little travelling abroad except for the odd 2 weeks on somewhere like the Costa del Sol. That was where Brits with good governmental connections were allowed to sun themselves periodically. Hetman had promised at least a few days in Paris or Amsterdam, both of which Harry would be keen to visit, having not been to either since he was a teenager;c) **interesting story**. Harry previously had never given much thought to the benefits and problems of being old in Britain. Like most people of his age group, he didn't naturally frequent places where the old gathered; and he had mentally and resolutely shut this group out of his mind's eye as he went through daily life. His own parents had died conveniently young – or at least his mother had; his father had long since disappeared out of the Woods family's life. But, he realised, there was an interesting story to be told, given the debate Hetman and his friends were going to launch;d) **editor strongly in favour.** Whatever Hetman had said to his Editor, it had clearly struck a chord. His Editor – while respecting Harry's rights to choose his own stories – had early this morning rung and made clear to Harry how strongly he would support 'going along with the Minister's wishes';e) **need a break from Carol**. Harry was slightly embarrassed about this entry. But there was no doubt that the sexually voracious Carol was becoming increasingly demanding of his time and energy. Harry had never seen himself as settling down with any woman. A month away would be enough to give him a little freedom, without burning any boats if his mind still turned to her when he got back.

Another 15 minutes produced a smaller and rather ambivalent list of 'minuses';i) **falling in with Hetman**. Well, it was true that Harry didn't like or trust Hetman. But provided Harry stuck to his guns, he could see no way in which Hetman could force him to do or write what he didn't want;ii) **outside my comfort zone**. Yes, it was true – as he had said to Hetman when they first met – that Harry didn't 'do' politics. But this wasn't really a political story and Harry had long felt that he needed to broaden his range of subjects if he were to stay at the top. Any final doubts on the appeal a story might have had been assuaged by a quick reflection. Young and old could be interested; iii) **being pushed around**. Well, that was just a variation on (i). Harry wasn't really being pushed around if he kept to his own agenda.

As was his custom, Harry spent another 30 minutes mulling over this list but could see no reason to change his initial conclusion – that he should say 'yes'. As a final check he tossed a coin – and was not surprised to find that, when it came down heads (i.e. that he should do it), his gut instinct agreed. Several times in the past Harry had failed to carry out a decision that his logical approach had steered him towards, because a toss of the coin at the end had somehow left him feeling the decision was 'not right'. But here, everything pointed the same way.

Harry then drew up a short ACTION list, which he went through with Simon by phone later that day. "*I shall want an office near you and secretarial/PA support. Cash up front for expenses. Access to your key officials who can tell me about the current 'Moving On' programme and the whole economic issue of old age as it currently is. Then I suggest we have the few days you have promised me in France or the Netherlands and round the month out with a couple of visits to your 'flagship' model towns for old folk. That way I get to see what is and could be here in England and be able to compare it with what happens in our near neighbours. I'm sure there'll be more as we go; but that's enough for starters.*"

Harry could tell from Simon's voice how relieved the latter was at Harry's decision. "*Hetman told me to provide you with whatever you needed so none of what you say is a problem. Weeks ago, Hetman had some of his key staff prepare briefing papers – on the basis I guess that you, or a substitute if you wouldn't do it, would want to see exactly what you've set out. Let's aim to start Monday. Bring your passport in so we can stamp it for access to France or the Netherlands. And clear your diary of everything for the foreseeable future. Welcome aboard, Harry".*

Simon finished on a note that Harry hadn't expected. *"By the way, of course you can have what secretarial and PA help you need. But Tara has agreed to help you get around abroad, so that will be someone from the 'get-go' who you know."*

When Harry rang off, he looked pensively down at the original paper on which he had written the pluses and minuses. After a brief period of thought, he added one word to both the plus and minus columns – 'Tara'. Yes she would be helpful but the less time with her the better.

He didn't pause long over this. He had promised Carol a good night out and had planned it so that she would have plenty of time to show him at the end how much she would welcome him back. In the event, thought Harry the next morning, she had been remarkably understanding about an enforced month out for the pair of them. Probably a good thing, he thought…on the whole.

6

LEARNING THE FACTS

"When my information changes, I alter my conclusions. What do you do, sir?"
– John Maynard Keynes is reputed to have said this around 1940 but the quotation is disputed.

Monday morning came all too quickly – some things don't change whatever you're doing. Harry turned up at the Interior Ministry reception desk around 9.30. Simon had clearly done his homework. By 10.30 Harry had been issued with photo ID that would get him into and round the building and an electronic card to finance his purchases at the canteen. He had also found his newly prepared office just down the corridor from Simon's own, together with a small adjacent room for a secretary, Hazel, who was sitting there ready – initially in a rather distant but polite way – for action. The phone was working; the whole place gave the aura of being ready to leap into action at his order.

Simon seemed to be in high spirits. *"You may not believe it but we bureaucrats can really move when circumstances – or someone like Hetman – demand. I've fixed up a couple of hundred pages of initial briefing for you to read, mostly stuff that Hetman commissioned a few months ago. I've got the*

21

2 main authors standing by to talk when you're ready. But, while I know of your reputed appetite for work, I think it will be a day or so before you surface. Oh and the coffee here is good, as is the restaurant which Hazel will take you to later."

Simon was in such a good mood that he didn't even argue when Harry explained that he thought he could manage without Tara, at least initially. *"Well, that's actually quite convenient with her as it happens given how little notice we've had. I'll fix up the visits to the South-West just for you. But she'll want to join you for your European trip."*

With that Simon withdrew, Harry pulled up his comfortable chair and – for the lack of a better plan – started at page 1 of the mound of briefing that had been piled on his desk. He soon established, to his slight relief, that the material was well written, co-ordinated and logically presented. He spent the rest of a long day with his head buried in the reading. By Tuesday lunchtime, when he mentally resurfaced for air, the main lines of the briefing were clear.

As was his wont. Harry summarised these main points on just a couple of sheets of paper.

Target of the new programmme:
About 10 million people over 65, of whom nearly half were over 75 and tens of thousands 90 or more.

Supposed Problem:
(Harry added the word 'supposed' which certainly hadn't been in the briefing). These people produced very little. Over half were dependent on State pensions and other benefits for most or all of their expenses. Health care costs were high and rising. The population was ageing rapidly – the number of people over 90 had doubled in

just 15 years. And the costs of providing adequate health facilities and carer support were also rising sharply. In some cases, it was argued that even finding and providing adequate resources, spread all round the country as they currently had to be, was proving near impossible to staff, let alone fund. None of the funding issues were new. Medical spending per head, across the whole population, had doubled between 1997 and 2010. It had risen further since then; and, while many of the older generation did not incur major costs until near the end of their life, some of the extension of life expectancy had undoubtedly been won at the cost of higher State spending.

How old people currently felt:
There were pages of statistics outlining an argument that most old people in the general population were lonely and unhappy. Things weren't too bad for the majority in their 70s who by and large had good health. Once they got to be over 90, most were said to have little or no contact with relatives and spent lonely worried lives – in contrast with what the authors described as prospectively a completely new lease of life in the new environment.

What had been done to date:
The existing 'Moving On' programme was described in the briefing as 'a start'. About 100,000 older people had been persuaded to sign up, sever their family and other links and move into the special towns – mostly in the south west – that the Government had built or sometimes refurbished. The briefing argued that better health care support could be provided there than among the general population for about 40% less money; and – if true thought Harry – it was claimed that over 70% of those who had moved were

said to be 'happy or very happy' with the change they had made. The existing programme could be scaled up without difficulty.

Proposal:
Hugely step up, over a couple of years, the programme for 'Moving On', with emphasis first on the over 80s but recognising that younger people were more likely to be willing to take the plunge. Do this with a mixture of carrot and stick. For carrots, the authors had suggested financial and practical components. Those moving could take what possessions they chose with them and be able to pass all the rest on, completely tax-free in wills the moment they moved. No more waiting for probate or lawyers' fees. Hetman was even willing to allow property to be sold without attracting stamp duty. Practically, promises would be made that standards of health care would be at least as good as – and more readily available than- in the rest of the country. And, a slightly but only slightly hidden stick, those choosing not to take up these offers would, in future, face increased direct and inheritance taxation on their income and assets. Nor would the Government promise that general health care standards would be maintained for those not moving; demand for health care otherwise would become 'overwhelming'.

As Harry laid down the last batch of paper, it occurred to him, not for the first time, just how amazingly simple a good bureaucrat could make hugely complex problems. Nevertheless, and Harry accepted this was reasonable, you had to reduce complex issues to their basics. And, if you got those right and, as importantly, knew where you wanted to go, the general thrust of what policy changes were needed could be established quite quickly. Harry did agree with what Hetman had said about the current government drifting without much vision. And he also agreed that, if people could be tied in to and motivated by big picture initiatives, you could achieve a great deal. He remembered dimly in his youth laughing at the efforts of politicians in the first 2 decades of the 21st Century to launch concepts like the Big Society, and the Inclusive Society. One big question for Harry was whether Hetman's ideas were just empty slogans as these earlier ideas had been or were they genuinely innovative, with real content.

7

THE CASE FOR CHANGE

By Tuesday lunchtime, Harry was in need of human company, other than Hazel who had been efficient and readily available when he needed something, but who was clearly not going to have real insights into what he needed to wrestle with. *"Could I talk to the 2 main authors of all this stuff I have been wading through, Claire McMahon and John Faulkner? One this afternoon, one tomorrow morning would be good."* Hazel made it clear that was no problem and, at 2 pm after a good but alcohol-free lunch in what was a decent in-house restaurant but which the staff insisted on calling 'the canteen', Claire duly appeared round the door.

Harry knew only too well how susceptible he was to a pretty face and he had developed quite a well-established technique to avoid allowing his views to be swayed when he found one. Claire was, to put it bluntly, gorgeous. Perhaps mid-30s, medium height, rounded features, lovely black hair artlessly/artfully combed to come round her left ear and trail down to shoulder level. A good figure from what the grey business suit and sharp white shirt showed; and a most delightful Irish brogue to go with it. All topped off with a bright neck scarf which somehow suggested that

26

here was a girl who could blossom at a moment's notice if the circumstances required or if the mood took her.

Harry let her sit in the chair on the other side of his desk. That prevented him from seeing her shapely legs, which Harry decided was just how it needed to be. *"Do please call me Claire. The Minister has told me why you are here. I can imagine you have a number of questions given that you've obviously read"* – she gesticulated at the paper on Harry's desk – *"most of what I've been working on in recent months".*

"Yes" replied Harry. *"Perhaps we could start with a little of your background so I can better understand your standing on these subjects." "Of course. Well, I trained as a doctor, practised as a GP for a few years and then decided that I could shape and move much more with a job like this. About that time I came to Mr. Hetman's attention – he was working in the Health Ministry then – and I regularly ended up on the opposite side of the table from him. He must have liked what he saw because – like John you'll meet later – he then hired me and has taken me with him as he has moved around since then. For the last 9 months or so, John and I have both worked full-time on Moving On."*

Harry belatedly offered Claire coffee, for which she thanked him but declined. *"So, in essence, much of the material in this briefing about the pressure of old age on health care, the costs and the associated benefits that might follow from these reforms come from you?"*

"They come," she replied rather acidly *"or at least the work on what life is like in the traditional sector comes from NHS documents and professional assessments, often by independent think-tanks. Much of it is unarguable. The stats on the ageing population and the linked health implications have been worrying those involved since the*

turn of the century. Long runs of data are readily available. Short of another plague epidemic or similar unknown, the trends of the age profile of the population have been clear and predictable for several decades; and, compared with most forecasts they are ones you could literally stake your life savings on. I suppose the only area in my work you could say is speculative is what I have written about the future. Personally, I think future cost pressures will be worse than forecast there because I really do think that the whole life-prolongation business abroad will impact us here a great deal. They are going to come up with major breakthroughs that will prolong life, albeit at a major cost. I really do think cures for dementia and most remaining types of cancer are well advanced abroad. While it probably won't be possible to roll back existing cases, I think that, in 10 years' time, new dementia or cancer cases will be a rarity on a parallel with TB or one of the other 19th Century killers.

Now obviously that's great news for those getting older; they will have a better quality of life for longer. But improvements will only come with a lot of State money to facilitate them. And, of course, a longer life span without a commensurate increase in private savings for retirement (of which there is no sign) means the income floor provided by the State will get drawn on more and more.

Given the controls we now have on foreign travel and on the flow of information from abroad, we can -if we wish – do something to slow down the spread of news of new 'cures'. We can also slow down the importation of the drugs that will no doubt be needed. But, Harry, you know perfectly well how news from abroad spreads – you yourself probably have excellent illegal channels for accessing such news. So of course word will spread. And what would any Government here do- have to do – if it becomes known that say 5 million people could take new expensive drugs now to ward off future dementia? The political pressure to act immediately would be huge and so would the pressure from the big pharma firms. The result – vast increases in spending and potentially life span – would be a foregone conclusion."

Harry let those thoughts rest in the air for a minute, a favourite trick of his. *"But how is Moving On going to help that? Whether these people are spread round the country or are all in the new model towns you want to build, they'll still get to hear of the innovations, they'll still want to have them. How is Moving On really going to help?"*

8

THE CASE FOR CHANGE – PART 2

No pleasure is worth giving up for the sake of two more years in a geriatric home in Weston-Super-Mare.
– Attributed to Kingsley Amis

Claire looked at him for a full minute. She eventually gave what sounded like a small sigh and began afresh. *"The Minister told me to be frank and brutally honest in talking to you, so that is exactly what I will do. And forgive me if it then sounds a little as though I am treating you as an idiot. It's not that. It's just that, like so many people, you have never really thought about this problem – indeed, you've probably done all you could never to think about it. So I need to make sure you really get it.*

Let me take one set of figures from my briefing. When a child is born there are of course considerable costs. For most healthy people they then need not much spent on them again all the time between 5 and 60, maybe up to 70+ with luck., They'll probably spend a lot more themselves on looking better, having corporate check-ups and the like; but that's no concern of the State. Then from 70 on, the aggregate costs start to soar as more of that age cohort goes sick. From there on, it gets worse for each year they age – more health spending from the State, more financial support needed as their own finances fail. We now have 1 million people between the ages of 90 and 100. My guess –we're trying to get decent figures that are all-encompassing- is that those over 90 cost the State about £10,000 a year. EACH.

Look at it another way. Half of all the health costs in an average person's life come in the last 6 months of that life. Happily, that 'last 6 months' now starts a good deal later than it did. But, even so, as soon as there is even a rumour of a new anti-cancer treatment or another even more expensive heart monitoring machine, the tabloids spread news of it and the jungle drums of the elderly, looking to use their voting influence on the Government, get going. So the total bill for us is huge, growing each year and can only be destined to get worse.

Now, suppose you have 20,000 people over 80 in a special town, having moved on. We can have a hospital dedicated to specifically what they need (no call for pregnancy services and the like). We can have specialists there who can be efficiently utilised because the need for their services can be predicted pretty accurately. We won't need extensive police or other mainline services – the main problem in the New Towns for any police will be finding old folk who've forgotten where they live. In short – and there are piles of stats in my work to back it up – we can cut costs by 30-40% compared with the costs if they stay in the general population AND we can give better services at the same time. I'll be frank. We can also slow down the spread of information about developments abroad for those who have Moved On – the agenda will be much more in our control. That's before we add in the benefit of the fact that the State owns the land and bought it cheap as part of the recovery programme *from the plague in the 20s; and (Hetman asked me to be totally frank) yes we can also save money and tap into scarce resources, because it's much easier politically to bring in Filipino and Polish nurses in these special towns than it would be in the rest of the country. As John will tell you tomorrow, actually finding enough British staff to man hospital and care services in most of England is a full-time headache, nearly impossible. If we didn't have this odd phenomenon that people in England don't seem to regard the Irish (like me!), Australians or South Africans as 'foreign' and therefore accept them readily, the Health Services in 'traditional England' would have collapsed years ago.*

Oh and one last political point that Hetman was anxious you understood. A million old people in new special towns will have at most 15 Members of Parliament. Of course, they will all favour all sorts of help for the elderly, paid for by the State. But, believe me, it's going to be hugely easier for the Government to live with the pressure from such a small number rather than, as now, having to accept that almost every MP across the country can be at the beck and call of a significant number of older voters. The elderly always top the voting averages – they really do turn out in numbers when their interests are at stake. So 15 MPs for the elderly against the 100 or more who currently worry, on every subject, what their older voters will want. If you were the Government which would you choose – even if there were no big cost savings to go with it?"

With that, Claire left Harry to his own devices. About an hour later, Harry closed the reading material (he had gone back over several aspects of Claire's written briefing) and made his way to the central London hotel where he had insisted Simon install him for the duration of this exercise. After a good bottle of Beaujolais and a fine steak,

Harry felt pretty satisfied with his first 2 days, even if, later, his dreams were disturbed by numbers leaping off the page and dancing around in his head. As they had danced when he had read Claire's work.

9

THE CASE FOR CHANGE – PART 3

We are born, we eat sweet potatoes and then we die.
–Easter Island Proverb.

Harry had decided that Wednesday, Day 3, could be allocated to John Faulkner and his briefing. That had quickly shown itself to be a lot less about money and big picture politics than Claire's had been. It very obviously and quickly got down to a long dissertation on what a poor deal the old were currently getting and how the system was failing their social and personal needs.

John's initial proposition was that, as the old aged, they became increasingly isolated from their family if they had one; and, as their own friends started to sicken or die off, they became isolated also from any real contact with *any* human being at all. So, for example, by the age of 75 most elderly people were seeing very little of their families though they still had active friends around. By the age of 90, contact with family was usually limited to a handful of occasions each year, and most friends were dead, ill or ailing. About 30% of people over 70 seemingly had no close family anyway.

John's second proposition was that, as people aged, they also became less physically and emotionally able to cope with the rough and tumble of normal living. For example, pages of stats on the old's fears of crime. John argued that these fears were greatly exaggerated if you believed the police's own data. But rumour and misreporting justified many old people adopting a life style of not going out at all at night or increasingly, as they aged, by day either even if physically able to do it. Several efforts had been made to get the true picture across but so far to little avail.

His third proposition was that, unarguably, roughly half of the elderly had little or no savings and were financially dependent on the limited help provided by the State pension and sometimes family. There was indeed a sizeable cohort of older people who regularly went abroad if allowed to and who could afford plenty of 'treats' to make life more enjoyable. But, by the age of 90, 75% of the elderly were left imagining a world in which they would only get frailer, Government would only get tougher with housing and carer benefits, and – except for the really wealthy –were unable to pay for specialist nursing care as and when it was needed.

So, John was able quite quickly to paint a picture of a large number of elderly people physically and emotionally isolated, in housing that was often unsuitable. Knowing that they had neither the human nor financial resources to cope with extended periods of ill health. One of John's favourite briefing ploys was to quote extensively from interviews carried out by charities and others interested in providing help. The pensioner who spent nearly all his waking hours travelling on buses, using his free bus pass – to keep warm in the winter but also to have something to do. The repeated comments from those who had lost all hope but who ruled out suicide for religious or practical reasons. One such comment, which Harry knew would come back to him from time to time for days, was the old woman who said *"I go to bed every night hoping I won't wake up in the morning."* And sadly that seemed to be a common thought, especially after a long-time (Harry supposed generally loved) spouse died. So many things in our society had changed in Harry's life time; but it seemed that some of the basic urges – warmth, safety, company were as great as ever – and increasingly not met in old age.

John's briefing also included lengthy 'evidence' from the two main bodies that were still, after several decades, trying to get the law changed to permit assisted suicide. After reading one piece dictated by a motor neurone patient who had been 'forced' to die a natural death, Harry felt almost physically sick. Harry cross-examined John (who appeared as normal and as reasonable as Claire had been the day before). And that evening, after just 3 days into the project, Harry accepted that Hetman's views certainly had foundation, even if he, Harry, had many questions and reservations. A lot of old people wanted to be allowed to die. A lot of medication and help was provided for people for whom the expense and effort did little to improve their quality of life. A lot of really elderly people just sat and suffered, alone and unloved.

10

OUT IN THE 'REAL WORLD'

'Old age isn't a battle; old age is a massacre' **Philip Roth**
'We are happier in many ways when we are old than when we are young. The young sow wild oats, the old grow sage.'

–**Winston Churchill**

Harry hadn't changed his underlying view three days later, as he led Carol into the hotel dining room for what she would undoubtedly regard as a treat and which he, even after 4 nights of eating there, certainly wouldn't have wanted to pass by. Hetman was putting him through the mill and the least Hetman could do, in return, was pay for Harry to have a bit of fun. Let the Ritz be the venue. Let Carol be the instrument. Let the evening begin.

Harry had spent the last 3 days visiting a selection of hospitals, old peoples' homes and old folk living alone in and around London. He had talked further with Claire and John and accepted their viewpoint that time was short and that the situation in the South East was in many ways better (because more affluent) than elsewhere in the country.

To limit the extent to which Claire and John could guide him where they wished, Harry had insisted on being given a list of available hospitals, one of old people's homes and a third of groups involved with the elderly from which he, Harry, picked at random. And it said a great deal, Harry thought, for Hetman's authority that nowhere had there been a refusal to meet with him despite the very short notice, or any sign that he was being given anything other than a straight view of what these people saw and felt. Harry also appreciated the car and driver Hetman laid on for him; as well, he had to admit, he appreciated the company and 'steering' round some difficult issues that Claire and John gave him when – as proved to be the norm – one of them travelled with Harry.

At the end of it, on Saturday just before Carol arrived, Harry had pulled out another of his blank sheets of paper and summarised what he had seen around 2 general columns that he labelled PULL and PUSH.

Under **PULL**, Harry noted the following: If they were well, people were generally content and living a decent quality of life until they were 70, sometimes considerably longer. But the older people get the more they felt lonely, the more they suffered from health issues, and, for quite a few, the more they would be happy to end it all in some rosy-hued 'nice' way. For many of this older group, dementia in some form had stepped in at some point and ironically made life more bearable, at the price generally of forgetting who they were or had been.

The poor were the worst off and indeed most of them enjoyed very little of what Harry would have called quality of life from about 70 on. While still independent, they often lived in unwelcoming accommodation and had neither the money nor the interests and ability to follow pursuits that could have lifted them. As life became more difficult and as friends died off and family members drifted away from the responsibility, many of this group ended up in state-run homes. These were the successors to the Local Authority-financed care homes of 20 years earlier. Harry shuddered at the thought of the couple of such homes he had visited, watching old people who spent 21 hours a day or more in bed or hunched in front of a television set, the seeming legions of older people who talked to themselves or to no-one. The richer did much better, according to their wealth. But, even for them, by the time they hit their late 80s one at least of each couple had usually 'had enough'. And they often feared what the future might bring.

Under **PUSH**, Harry noted that the health sector clearly found the elderly a great strain. He thought back to the GP who had railed about the number and demands of his elderly patients and who clearly and probably unreasonably had laid every one of his frustrations at the door of the elderly. He also recalled the little scene he had witnessed in one hospital of an 85 year old lying in bed surrounded by a doctor, a nurse, a local authority official and another bureaucrat. The group had desperately needed to empty beds, to make room for new patients. They were trying to establish whether the old man had any family or other help who could be relied on to provide support if this man went home. Questions rained in on the old man who, Harry had concluded within 2 minutes, had no idea of who or where he really was – and certainly no ability to describe accurately who or what might be waiting for him at home. And yet, in the end the group had concluded that he could indeed go home, so great obviously was the pressure on hospital beds.

After a little thought, Harry also wrote down 4 more words in capitals – **NO MONEY, BETTER USES**. From many things he had done before, Harry knew only too well how stretched Government financial resources were; and just how many (and often justified) were the hands reaching out for any spare cash that might be available. He could readily understand how someone like Hetman would have many alternative uses for any money saved.

Of course, Harry noted to himself, to lighten his mood, there were obviously many exceptions. He remembered one lovely old couple who could still get around and who for 50 years had enjoyed ballroom dancing together and still did. He also recalled the man of 95 who had enough money to afford his own mobility buggy and whose mind had been as sharp as a needle. Harry had also drawn some real comfort from the fact that many of the medical staff and carers seemed genuinely to have the interests of their elderly charges at heart. No doubt there were cases of abuse and ill treatment; that was the kind of thing TV companies and others liked to highlight. But, Harry thought, in typically English fashion the system had so far muddled through as best it could.

There was certainly none of what a consultant would have called 'low-hanging fruit' – changes that could be recommended that could save a significant amount of money with relatively little pain. Indeed, Harry could see enough of the picture to think there probably wasn't much high, inaccessible fruit either, without radical change. Hetman was at least right in asserting that, if something substantial needed to be done, it was going to take some genuinely new thinking.

11

NEWHOME

"Human beings are perhaps never more frightening than when they are convinced beyond doubt that they are right."
   – Laurens van der Post The Lost World of the Kalahari.

A pleasant Saturday night and Sunday spent with Carol meant that, by early Monday, Harry's mood had lightened. This was the week where Simon's people had promised that Harry could visit a couple of the 'new towns' that had been created in the last few years to house the first of those who had 'Moved On'.

John appeared at the hotel around 9 a.m. and collected Harry, who had been told to bring a bag with overnight things and a couple of changes of clothes. John – in contrast to Harry – seemed in more pensive mood this week. *"Listen Harry. I need to tell you a bit about these towns and what I've arranged for you. The towns are basically of 2 types. The first were sea-side spots – mostly in Devon and Cornwall – villages that already existed and were badly hit by the fall-off in demand from the effects of the plague and when foreign tourists started avoiding the UK. The Government of the day – Hetman isn't right if he thinks that he is the first progressive Minister – stepped in. With a mixture of buying*

41

in a depressed market and compulsory purchase orders, the Government was able to create a number of little townships which already had infrastructure, buildings and the rest, that could then be used to build up a new town suited only to the elderly. Generally a hospital had to be put in. But otherwise most of the things needed were there or could be adapted cheaply. Lots of attractive sea-view apartments without a doubt. And virtually no cars – except for local public transport – so loads of converted garages and the like.

The other 'source' of new towns was from buying up land – mostly golf courses I believe – and building everything from scratch. Not so cheap or so quick but at least that allowed the planners to create a purpose-built small town in its entirety. What has happened since has been a bit of learning by doing and making changes that became obvious. For example, it rapidly became clear that it was cheaper and better to have most of the really elderly and all those with, say, dementia in one place, not scattered over several towns. What typically happens now is that someone moves on and, if they are in good health, starts off in one of the centres where they have space. If they want, people can have their own allotments – several of these places grow much of the vegetables and fruit they need. Then, as people age or become infirm, they are encouraged to move to somewhere more suited for them.

There is still plenty of free land left, which Hetman and his friends can quickly develop to house a wave of new 'movers'. I know he is thinking of a 5 year programme to house at least 1 million new residents, most of that tailored towards the end of the period and the very elderly. *But there can be plenty more after that."*

By this time, Harry and John were together in the back seat of the car, heading Harry knew not where. John leant forward. *"You have to approach all this with an open mind,*

Harry. The first time I went to one of these places, my first reaction was not wholly positive. But you have to bear in mind – and contrast it with – how these people would be living in 'normal life'. We are going to start you off in one of the places for the younger and fitter, then move you down the coast to one of the established sea-side towns that caters for the really elderly. In each case, you'll be in the hands of the local Village manager. Of course, you will be welcome to ask him or her for what you want. We'll come back for you on Friday."

That was how Harry found himself taking off in a helicopter, from Northolt, about 11.00 that morning. Harry had no great liking for flying in helicopters; but, while he had no idea what kind of aircraft it was, he noted with some relief that it was one of those with 2 rotors not one. Probably not true but he always felt that the second small rotor at the back gave them a chance if something went wrong with the main propulsion unit. There was no delay or bureaucracy – Hetman's people had clearly prepared the ground well.

Harry found himself sitting on one of 6 seats in the plane, with Maria, a no-nonsense mousey-haired young woman of maybe 25, who turned out to be one of John's assistants and who obviously worshipped the ground on which he walked. The other seats were empty; but, as Maria explained, the helicopter often carried just a few people down to the West Country along with the substantial supplies (typically medicines or food) that she said was normally the main cargo.

Harry tried to pump Maria for information. But it turned out that she herself had never been into one of the New Towns; this was a first for her. As she explained *"You'll see that access to and from the towns is tightly controlled*

– has to be just in case someone gets it into their head to revisit old memories back East. I just handle some of the purchases for stuff to be flown down – things like that. I'm having a day down there to meet the people who run that end of the organization and get to see how it works."

They flew to what had been Newquay. Maria commented that the airfield here was a good example of how they had managed to reengineer the previous infrastructure at little cost. *"Newquay used to have internal tourist flights from places like Gatwick. So it already had storage space and roads away from it that we can now use completely differently. And 4 or 5 of our New Towns are within 30 miles."*

The journey took about 2 hours and passed without incident. Climbing down the steps on arrival, Harry was met by a tall thin individual of maybe 40, who introduced himself as Carl Jones, manager of the New Town that had once been Wadebridge. Carl was clearly in the mood to make Harry feel welcome – no doubt, Harry thought, on instructions from London. Harry sniffed the air appreciatively. The sea wasn't in sight but that familiar tang, which immediately brought back some generally positive memories from his childhood, was unmistakeable and welcome. The sky was broadly clear of clouds and the sun shone intermittently. A typically nice day for mid-September, made more enjoyable by the knowledge that the weather was bound to turn soon.

Introductions made, Harry's modest bag was quickly gathered and put into a saloon car. Carl obviously merited a driver and, as the driver quickly accelerated up what Carl explained had once been the A38, Carl and Harry sat together in the back seat.

"We kept some names but also changed a lot too,

often asking the first arrivals to choose names they were comfortable with" said Carl. "Now, let me just explain the plan. We aim for you to be here until sometime on Wednesday, at which point we'll transfer you to one of the larger villages given over to the old and sick. We'll get to the Town now – we call it Newhome for obvious reasons, not its original name I need hardly add. Actually, some smart-ass originally wanted to call it Newholme; but the first residents voted to drop the 'l'.

I've got a late lunch for you at my admin HQ and I'll then take you on a short tour of the town. We only have about 15,000 people so a tour doesn't take long. Then I'll drop you at the one remaining hotel we've kept open for visitors like you from London. I'm afraid you shouldn't expect great standards of service. But the food is quite good, the building's main purpose is to be one of the 3 or 4 decent restaurants we've ensured would survive. And they've been told to be at your beck and call.

The journey took only about 25 minutes; there was hardly another vehicle on the road, which Harry deduced must make for a pretty cheap local road repair service. The only hold-up was about a mile out of Newhome, where the car stopped at what turned out to be a checkpoint, manned by men who looked military and were dressed in fatigues.

"We have an electronic perimeter for the town which no-one can go outside without permission. But only a couple of manned checkpoints like this, so not a great need for resources. If there is a dementia case we haven't picked up and they go wandering, the perimeter will often keep them in. If, as I'm afraid is very occasionally the case, a resident decides they want to go back to old stamping grounds and revoke their signing up to 'Moving On', the perimeter isn't an effective restraint. But it does tell us someone has gone

where they shouldn't. We then rely on the fact that the individual will have little idea where they are, they will have no money useable in the East or contacts; and there are no tourists or civilians around for miles who might be conned into helping them."

Harry consciously looked hard at Carl. *"Does this happen often?" "There have been about 50 cases in the 5 years I have been here."* replied Carl *"usually linked to something like the 18th birthday of a favourite grandchild or maybe an important date for the individual, like the anniversary of their Moving On." "Anyone ever succeeded?"* asked Harry. *"Not as far as we know"* replied Carl with what seemed to Harry like a forced smile. *"We notice the disappearance of anyone quickly. And most people here anyway are quite willing to wear a GPS-tag in case they get lost. A couple of times we have had a temporary 'loss' of an individual but that sadly has always been made good by finding that the person has keeled over and died while out on a walk or at their allotment. So I think –like everywhere else round here – we can claim a 100% attendance record."*

Harry realised that this last subject seemed to have put Carl a little out of sorts; and, after brief reflection, Harry dropped the subject – for now, he assured himself. No-one likes to be reminded that they – and their systems – are only human. Carl was definitely human.

12

SETTLING IN

"Home is the place where, when you have to go there, they have to take you in."
–Robert Frost The death of the hired man.'

Carl kept to the timetable he had outlined to Harry. A perfectly respectable sandwich lunch was followed by a tour by car and on foot of Newhome, which took about 90 minutes. Not surprisingly, Carl could reel off lists of statistics on almost anything that Harry asked about. And of course most of the statistics were 'points for the plus column'. One thing that Carl returned to again and again was how easy (and cheap) it had been to turn what was already there when they arrived to a different use. So, for example, the one cinema had been left as was, likewise the main supermarkets round the town and a selection of the main restaurants. The road system had been perfectly adequate; and now only the occasional worker boasted a car. Unusually for that part of Cornwall there was no proper beach access but, for example, the old Camel trail had been left for bikers, at least up to the perimeter. Quite a lot of commercial premises had been gutted or transformed – *"we didn't need estate agents did we nor endless bank and building society branches? We also didn't need any schools—this is a child-free area and we don't hire workers who have children. And think of all those garages we could turn into sheds for people to potter in."*

About the only serious expenditures Carl explained had been on a new hospital on the edge of town and on the new 'protection circle' as Carl insisted on calling the perimeter fence.

Harry asked as tactfully as he could *"Well, how do people live then? They arrive having moved on. You presumably process them and allocate them accommodation? You give them some kind of induction? And then what? How do they buy food and necessities? How are they able to enjoy themselves on the wife's birthday or for a drink on a Friday night? How does their daily life 'tick'?"*

Carl gathered his thoughts very quickly. *"Well, some of it is quite easy. New arrivals get some induction preparation before they come. Then, when they get here, we pair each newcomer or couple off with an existing inhabitant who gets paid a small amount for showing them the ropes and the town. A lot of those relationships end in close friendships I'm pleased to say. We allocate them to a nursing practice (our doctors are all based in the hospital – most of the preliminary work can be done by nurses much more cheaply). And we also allocate them a dentist. Then – and going forward – it's all much easier than it would have been back East.*

As for 'living', we have our own local money and each person gets a basic allowance of 250 Newhome pounds a week plus anything they earn on top or convert from money from back East that they have brought with them. That's instead of their pension, rent allowance and other things they would have claimed back East. No borrowing, no credit cards, no mortgages or utility bills. You can wander round the shops and the 2 things you will be struck by, I guess, are how cheap basic necessities are; and that – by comparison with back East – the choice is limited, which is one of the ways we keep the prices down. We worked out early on that there was no point in offering 10 different kinds of champagne in the drink stores or 12 types of toilet paper. And, perhaps the oddest thing you'll hear, there is almost NEVER a price increase on an item. The prices here are generally what they were, translated into Newhome pounds, when we started. Makes life a whole lot easier and less stressful for the older people here, believe me. Dealing with the real world effects of price rises is done by us; the inhabitants don't have to worry; indeed they have precious little to worry about at all. "

"Sounds great but I'm sure there has to be a lot of paddling under the water by you guys to keep things going smoothly. And working? What can people do and how?" asked Harry, trying to show it was meant as a friendly question. *"Well"* replied Carl *"we pay people for things we want. So you can earn 100 Newhome pounds by taking on an arriving couple. If you're up to a bit of waiting, we pay 7 new pounds an hour for barmen and waiters – surprisingly popular that is, though there aren't many vacancies. We pay – I think it's about 5 pounds an hour for people working on the fruit and vegetable allotments. And so on. Most people start out with at least one part time job – good for them and us. Then, as they get older, their financial needs and their willingness to devote energy to such jobs both tend to fall away."*

"How many outside staff do you have and where do they come from?" asked Harry. *"There must be a lot of jobs on top of medical and the like where younger able-bodied experts are needed."*

Carl paused before launching into his reply. *"I guess about 600 in all. We have about 20 police for internal security – we don't exactly face a crime wave apart from breaking up the odd domestic row. We have about 100 nurses and maybe 80 doctors and dentists. Add in the odd chef, IT guys- and bus drivers – we have a great local service so people don't notice their lack of a car. We also need repair and maintenance people, mostly plumbers and handymen (though any major work here gets sub-contracted) and you get to about 600 which is a fraction of what you'd find back East. Don't forget, though"* added Carl *"we don't have people who are chronically sick or need major care. You'll find a lot of them when you move on from here. Those people take considerably higher support ratios. The other thing I should say up front –you'll see it for yourself soon enough – is that many of these 600 except for security are foreign; cheap, reliable and – unlike back East – no-one here seems to resent them being around because they don't compete for housing, education or health resources. We don't have any trouble filling the jobs, that's for sure."*

As Carl finished speaking, the car drew up on the High Street outside what Harry saw was described as 'The one and only hotel'. *"That's exactly what it is"* said Carl following the direction of Harry's stare. *"Most of the time we don't need any of its rooms and it serves as a major party function unit. I'll introduce you to the manager who is one of the 600 and he'll make sure you're fed and cared for. Don't expect 5 star- or indeed much service – the few 'staff around will be those inhabitants I told you about on 7 pounds an hour. But the food will be OK – they have a decent restaurant and Gorgi the manager will look after you. Your bill – including food and drink – is covered thanks to Mr Hetman. Here's 500 pounds of our local currency so you can try for yourself how the shops work.*

With that, Carl got out, went round the car, opened the door for Harry to get out and took him off to find Gorgi.

13

HARRY'S NIGHT OUT

"Be not forgetful to entertain strangers; for thereby some have entertained angels unawares."
–Hebrews Chapter 13 Verse 2

Giorgi turned out to be a thick-set, small but powerful man, who said he came from Romania but had worked here in England for 5 years. He seemed hardly overjoyed to have Harry staying with him; but he had been prepared well enough and led Harry quickly up to the second floor. *"You're our only visitor so you can have what was once the bridal suite. And if you don't like that, you can have any other room provided you don't mind the dust and make up the bed in it yourself. The main bar opens at 6 and I've allocated you a table for about 7.30. Make yourself at home – there should be plenty of hot water. Anything you need come down and find me."*

It was just after 5.00 by now and Harry had had a long enough day to want to relax and review his impressions so far. He would have to formulate a plan of campaign for the next day, as Carl had made it clear that – absent a real problem – he would be leaving Harry alone to go where he chose and do what he wanted to do. Harry found and ran a large old- fashioned bath and treated himself to a couple of bath tablets lying on the side. He lay back in the water. In spite of his priors, Harry had to admit that he had been impressed by much of what he had seen today. The simplification of daily life that was seemingly offered to people here, he could see, might well appeal to them. He would have to follow up intensively on what they could and did buy and what they did with their time. But, reviewing it, he could see that the arrangements avoided or short-circuited most of the stresses of daily life back East (as he himself was beginning to think of it). If the costs really did stack up the way John and now Carl had claimed, it might indeed be a very attractive option for all but the wealthiest older people back home.

Around 6.10 Harry walked down to the Ground Floor and followed the signs to 'The Bar'. About 20 people – he wasn't surprised to see they were all men – were there already and there was a steady buzz of conversation. He ordered a large gin and tonic – the barman waved away his offer of some of the Newhome pounds he now had, saying laconically *"I know who you are and that your bill is being taken care of."*

A corner table with 2 chairs was free and he made his way over and sat looking out into the room. He promised himself he would relax with the g & t and then put himself around and talk to some of the locals. But it was actually 2 g & ts before he felt like doing that, by which time the bar had filled up and become as full as he would have wanted to see it if he had been there of his own volition. Not surprisingly every man was visibly elderly – there were now a few women as well and one or two of these were quite young.

When he did finally push his chair back and join the nearest group of men, it was already nearly 7. He quickly discovered 2 things; first that people didn't seem to mind him striking up a conversation and second that it was 'party night'. This, it turned out courtesy of one of the locals, happened once a week; and it involved free drinks plus a 3 course meal and a bit of music – one man said 'sing-song" afterwards, all for 20 pounds.

As his main interlocutor added *"the sing-song is really only for those who haven't scored by then."* Harry did a quick mental double-take. Maybe half the men looked like they both knew what scoring entailed and like they might be up to their side of the bargain. But given the number of women he could see that were reasonably young, the odds didn't seem very promising, even for the men who could and might.

At 7.30, Giorgi appeared and announced that dinner was ready. It was obvious from the look he flashed at Harry that this was probably his only chance to eat too. As Harry looked around to see what he might do next, a woman's arm snaked under his left elbow; and an attractive female voice said quietly *"Do let me eat with you. I can't stand these things but I have to come and you look like a bit more fun than the rest."* Harry looked at the speaker as best he could, not easy given how close she had sidled up to him; and he was relieved to find that she was what Harry would describe as the right side of 40, probably 35, with nice make-up and hair. What he could see of her figure looked good too. His immediate 'take' had been that somehow Carol had wangled her way down to the West Country to join him. But this woman, who introduced herself as Ingrid, was very much alive and real in her own right, still hanging on to his arm. *"Delighted"* he heard himself say and they followed the 40 or so people now spilling into what turned out to be the dining room.

Giorgi avoided any difficulty there might have been by appearing at Harry's right hand and steering the pair to a modest table for 2 in the far left-hand corner. There were a couple of other small tables, together with 4 longer trestles which most of the men made straight for. The two handfuls of women tagged along behind the men and made sure that they sat together in pairs or the odd threesome, on one of the main tables. Obviously most of those present had done this many times before; and surprisingly quickly everyone was seated.

Harry took the chance, once he had sat down, to get a proper look at Ingrid who, in turn, was looking around as though checking off that one or two men were there who *should* have been there. Harry thought, now he had a better look, that she was indeed perhaps 35, slim and with attractive dark wavy hair and definitely made up for a night out. She turned her gaze on him and smiled attractively. *"I'm sorry for having picked you up like that. But there are several men here who I find objectionable and I thought you – as an obvious 'outsider' – would be a good way of keeping them off if I joined up with you. Anyway, as I said you look like fun. Now, who are you and what are you doing in this home for the elderly?"*

Harry was slightly shaken by her tone, which was so out of kilter with the days of positive briefing he had been receiving up to now. *"Well, I'm Harry Woods. I'm a journalist in the real world; and let's say just that I'm here to have a quick look round a typical town for Moving On."* Harry had no intention of saying more than that about his mission; but he had thought it over beforehand and had decided then that the line he was now taking was relatively safe if he were asked. It was true enough for his questions and interest to be explicable. And, the key point,

54

it explained why he – as a relatively young man – was there at all.

"*So you can get out of here when you want, can you?*" she said. "*Lucky you. I've had nearly a month in this and similar dumps up and down the coast. No choice.*" "*But what do you do?*" asked Harry. "*You'll see*" she replied as though that was an answer. And she looked down as a mixed salad – obviously meant to be the first course – was thrust under her nose.

"*You may have been warned that service standards here leave a lot to be desired*" commented Ingrid "*But I have to say I eat better at dos like this than I can otherwise here. And certainly for PDP celebrations like this the alcohol's usually OK too, in quantity and sometimes quality.*" "*What do you mean?*" asked Harry. "*What's a PDP party got to do with us here?*"

"*What do you think this is?*" replied Ingrid. "*These people have got the PDP to thank for virtually everything. Most of them – the men at least – were high-ranking officials in the PDP when they were still working. And there's actually great loyalty to the party here. So there's a weekly party*" "*What about the women?*" asked Harry. "*If they're over 60 they're wives of these officials or women who held a powerful job in their own right. If they're obviously younger, they're some of the East European or Asian women brought in to provide a few home comforts the old men can't get at home.*" Ingrid replied matter-of –factly. "*Hell*" replied Harry, really talking to himself. "*Carl didn't mention them among his 600 outside workers! And do you mean this is some kind of privileged town? That not everyone down here gets treated like this?*" Ingrid thought for a moment. "*Couldn't say. All I can tell you is that I've seen 4 towns down here, and a handful elsewhere, all like this. I've never seen anything different. But certainly, if there are more places down here, they don't merit a visit from me."*

This had given Harry some rather indigestible food for thought; and the 2 of them lapsed into silence while the salad was consumed. Fortunately, it quickly appeared that this was one of the evenings where the wine would flow reasonably freely (Harry now, in the light of what Ingrid had said, couldn't help but wonder if that was partly for his benefit). With a strong effort, Harry began some deliberately light conversation, the main aim of which – other than to fill a void – was to find out more about his new companion.

After a passable main course of chicken, dauphinoise potatoes and greens, together with 2 glasses of a decent Rioja, Harry was *a little* wiser. Ingrid had been born Elouise *"Ingrid is my stage name"*. A brief marriage had been terminated quickly with no children to worry about. *"And now I make my living – such as it is – out of the cabaret circuit. As I'm down here for a month you can work out for yourself how good the circuit is. Anyway, some PDP bigwig pressured me to do this; and you don't want to upset people like that."*

As the third course – a millefeuille pastry with raspberries (local no doubt) – appeared, Ingrid swallowed half a glass of Rioja and slid out of her seat. *"I've got to go and put my glad rags on"* she said. *"Pudding and you can wait till later."*

Harry sat, finished the dessert and his own wine and wondered what he should do. But that decision was largely taken out of his hands by Giorgi reappearing some 10 minutes after Ingrid had left and announcing through a formidable-looking microphone *"And now ladies and gentlemen, it's time to move onto the Ballroom where your entertainment awaits.*" With that, the men in the room as a body rose with full glasses where possible and decamped to the Ballroom, which turned out to be a biggish room next door. It had décor and lights that had probably been the height of fashion around 2000 but which now looked sad, and more than a little battered. Harry thought it was just as well the lighting was low. He moved with the mass of bodies, taking up a position, standing, near the left-hand wall. Again, he noted that most of the women still kept together, though one or two seemed to have peeled off after dinner and now definitely had male company.

At the far end of the room, a 5 man jazz band was playing. Harry quickly guessed from the limited quality of what he could hear that the band was probably made up from residents. But they were playing classics of the kind almost everyone would know and the effect was cheerful enough.

There followed a set of about 20 minutes, at the end of which Giorgi appeared with his microphone and thanked what turned out to be called the Dave Brubeck Memorial Band. "*And now*" Giorgi continued "*I bring you – straight from London and chosen for you personally by one of the most senior PDP Ministers back there – our top of the bill tonight. Let's hear it for Ingrid!*"

Some reasonably substantial applause followed which, within 5 seconds had turned into the kind of wolf-whistling that Harry would normally associate with a building site. As soon as Giorgi had made the introduction, Ingrid had glided into the room, now dressed – if it could be called dressed – in what Harry could only think of as a US cheerleader's outfit. Tight stockings, short skirt, even tighter figure-hugging blouse, thigh-length boots and a little black master of ceremonies jacket with tails hanging down at the back. She had slapped on a lot more make-up since Harry had sat with her; and the ensemble was completed with a top hat and a black and white cane.

She had the room – at least the men – riveted from the moment she appeared and mounted the little stage. *"Hello boys"*, *"Hello Ingrid"* most of the men roared back; and she was away.

Over the next 30 minutes, Harry heard funnier and much cruder jokes than he could remember having heard for a very long time. She sang 3 short rather 'blue' numbers to great appreciation. She used the hat and walking cane for things that they had never been intended for. And, by the end of half an hour, her costume had been reduced to a skimpy bra and dark red thong. Much of the humour entailed taking the piss out of the men there *"You're old, I'm busty, is your prick a little rusty..?"* was one of the few lines Harry could recall the next morning. There had been a lot more. But, and he was biased because he could see now just how attractive she could make herself, Harry had to accept that the male audience loved every minute.

When she finally called a halt and disappeared, there was a sudden silence and then huge stamping and whistling from all round the room. Giorgi had obviously been ready and, on that signal, half a dozen elderly waiters walked in and distributed as much wine as people's glasses would hold – all in the space of perhaps a minute. Full bottles of beer were left ostentatiously on side tables. And, once the men had realised they had seen the last of Ingrid for the night, the noise subsided and some serious drinking began.

Harry quickly put out of his mind any idea of following up his earlier conversations to find out more about life in Newhome. This just wasn't the time or place. He emptied his own glass – which had been refreshed along with all the others – and decided to slide quietly out of the room. As he was the only guest, he thought he must have a good chance of getting away upstairs unchallenged. And indeed – until he was standing outside his room looking for the key – his one 'problem' had been being almost trampled on the nearly dark stairs by a hulking oaf of a man. The latter had been hauling along behind him a pretty and visibly frightened little Filipino girl and very obviously looking for an empty room to enjoy himself.

For 5 seconds Harry thought of saying something but quickly thought much better of it – none of his business. He turned in the semi-darkness to his own door, the key had finally been located in his right-hand pocket – no easy job after 4 large glasses of Rioja. Just as the key turned, an arm slipped into his and the same husky voice he had heard earlier was speaking urgently into his ear. *"That was just one of the men I need to avoid. Save a girl if you can't save a soul Harry; and let me join you for a nightcap until the coast is clear."*

Without a word, he let them both into his room and shut the door quickly. She moved immediately into his arms and kissed him, covering every part of Harry she touched with cosmetics. *"Thank you, Harry. You won't regret it."* Somehow, he thought she was probably going to be right, though he did quickly offer her the towel from his bathroom to reduce the cosmetics flow to manageable proportions.

14

NEWHOME

"What's in a name? A rose by any other name would smell as sweet."

–William Shakespeare Romeo & Juliet

Harry wasn't a prude and he wasn't exactly inexperienced. But, when he came to review things the next morning, he was still amazed to find how much he had enjoyed that night and how little he had been in control of what happened. As soon as he had acquiesced to her staying, she kissed him with such intensity and verve that he could, at that point, already have forecast much of what subsequently happened. *"Don't worry that there isn't a mini-bar or room service. I provide my own booze at times like this."* she said to him. And indeed within 2 minutes they were seated with her on his lap, drinking brandy she had produced as if by magic, out of 2 tumblers she had found in the bathroom.

Ingrid had put some clothes back on since her stage performance, though as soon as Harry started to run his hands over her body, he realised that she still wasn't exactly overdressed. Harry took comfort from the fact that he (and he had already established that she) had no 'entanglements'. And, as went with who and what he was, he knew that, as usual, there were condoms ready to hand in his luggage . Nevertheless, he was still taken by surprise by the speed and efficiency with which she undressed him; and the enthusiasm with which she approached the act of love making. They said very little, there really was no need. And Harry, as was his wont, wasn't going to argue with what seemed like a huge stroke of fortune in bumping into and being with Ingrid. After all, he was obviously saving her from what she obviously regarded as a much worse fate; and she was saving him from boredom, which, to Harry, was one of the deadliest of sins if he was the one being bored.

So it was about 8 am the next morning that Harry found himself sitting up in bed and trying to reflect on what had happened. Ingrid had slipped out of the sheets around 7.30, dressed quickly and gone. *"I shouldn't really have stayed last night"* she said. *"But you were fun and I'll just get out of here before too many people are up and around. Thank God I haven't got another show to do until tomorrow."* Harry protested mildly. He sensed immediately that she would scorn the offer of any of the Newhome pounds he had – if that had been an issue, the subject would have come up at the start of the action last night. *"Shall I see you again?"* he asked. *"Not here"* she replied. *"If you ever fancy another fun evening, use your journalistic skills – if you are indeed a journalist– and track down 'Ingrid in Essex'. I shouldn't be too hard to find."* And, with that, she leant over the bed, quickly kissed him and was gone.

Harry decided that, if he wanted breakfast, he had better go down and look for it, which he did shortly after another hot bath. Giorgi's tuneless whistling led Harry quickly to a sizeable kitchen with a couple of high stools and a central fixture to sit at. Giorgi without a word pushed a large mug of coffee at him and a glass of orange juice; then, 5 minutes later, unasked, a plate of sausage, bacon and egg which Harry devoured very happily.

"Enjoyed yourself last night?" grunted Giorgi. *"I assume so from the effect you seemed to be having on our leading lady. Not that I'm jealous you understand. Live and let live round here. I was told you'd be out and around today and then back again this evening. No party tonight, so it would be good if you could be back to eat by 8. Carl's driver said he'd be round when I called him to say you had appeared. I'll do that now."*

Harry would have liked to ask Giorgi some questions but, now Giorgi knew how he'd spent his night, Harry didn't like to begin any significant line of interrogation. *"That would be great, Giorgi. How would you suggest I spend my time today?"* *"Well"* the man replied, looking fixedly at the coffee percolator he was refilling *"I guess the best thing would be to hit a couple of the halls where groups gather and talk to them there, if that's what you need to do. Carl's driver will know where to find a tai chi class or pilates for the under 70s – something that might not drive you nuts. And then you can catch a selection of residents on their home ground as it were."* Harry was so impressed with that analysis that all he said was *"That sounds a good idea."* And Harry wondered, as he had done before, just how much briefing Giorgi had had from Carl before Harry had arrived.

Thus it was that Carl's driver, Jeff, appeared outside the hotel just after 9.30. And Harry talked through how the day might go. *"Giorgi thought you might be able to take me to a couple of the halls where people gather to follow their hobbies. That sounds a good idea. I'd also like to go out and find a few of the people working – say on the allotments. And I want to go and spend a fair bit of time in a couple of big shops, seeing just what people can shop for and what they have to pay for the privilege. All done before getting back here early evening."*

Jeff agreed that this was a reasonable timetable to aim for; and, over the day, he proved a knowledgeable guide to the more practical sides of Newhome. They started in a school that had been converted into a day centre and Harry sat in on several of the morning events – based, as far as he could see around the principle of encouraging physical activity, such as tai chi or fairly gentle aerobics. He found people surprisingly relaxed when he invited them to join him for a hot drink to chat about how they found life. The only difficulty for him was the speed (or rather lack of it) at which life there moved, So even organising a dozen people to have a hot drink and sit round to chat with him took about 15 minutes. It also proved something of a strain to keep the conversation focused where Harry wanted it.

Not everyone gave the Newhome set-up 10 out of 10. But Harry was surprised how limited and even shallow many of the criticisms were. Wherever possible, he invited his interlocutors to compare life now with what it had been like back East. And generally, the conclusions were pretty favourable to being here. People actually liked the fact that there were no youngsters around. As one put it *"I never went out after dark back East. Here there is no crime to speak of, very little to worry about at all."* The medical facilities were generally praised and most of the adverse comments were around the difficulties of sometimes making ends meet or of a lack of choice in the shops. But even here, many comments were favourable. *"I don't have to meet unexpected utility bills, dental repair costs and so on. So I know what I've got to spend. I'm not surrounded by young people showing off their earning power. I won't get rung up by some fraudster trying to part me from my money. Life is very comfortable, very unthreatening, all said and done. There is plenty I can do if I want to; but no-one hanging round nagging me to do this or that."*

As delicately as he could, Harry raised the question of whether people missed their families. The immediate reply came from a relatively (by comparison) young man: *"Of course, most of us miss a few people, especially when we first arrive. But you'd be surprised how many people here didn't really have family that amounted to very much; and, for the rest, they can at least relax knowing that those left behind are getting the benefits of their money straight away. Anyway, it's not as though we have absolutely no contact. Some of us get the odd message from back East; and most of us know at least one of the workers who is prepared to take an occasional family message back East, when they go on leave – for a bit of cash of course. The authorities know all about it, they don't care, though someone seems to make sure that messages back are limited. Live and let live, that's the basic motto round here. And it works pretty well."*

If Hetman or Carl had somehow engineered a group of people here to give him a positive story, Harry had to admit that it had been so subtly done that he at least believed what he was hearing. Looking back, in the evening, Harry found he had written down only 2 possibly negative conclusions. The first was that most of the younger over-60s he talked to did work part-time; but they seemed unfazed by that or actually to welcome something to do. (This conclusion had been confirmed when Harry visited some of the allotments; those working there seemed to revel in what they were doing.) The second, much more concerning, point to his mind was that, as with the party the previous evening, there seemed a preponderance of old ex-PDP officials in the group. What did happen to 'normal people'? Where were they? Or was he seeing a problem that didn't exist?

On this last point, no-one could enlighten him. The people he spoke to didn't respond to the point when he made it; and none of them claimed to have experience of any town other than Newhome. They had arrived there from back East and stayed. The only move they could envisage was to what they referred to as 'the rest home' – which Harry established meant the places that people were moved to when they became too frail for normal life here or started to show signs of dementia.

Harry's prolonged visit to a supermarket yielded little more insight. The manager – one of the 600 'workers' – briefed him on arrival and Harry was then left to wander the shop and talk to customers as he chose. Harry did detect that the range of choice was much more limited than he saw back East. But prices seemed very reasonable and Harry realised he had seen no visible beggars or any 'down and outs' in his wanderings – something you could never say for London or any big city he knew of! And what was on sale was there in quantity. Again, Harry knew that wasn't always the case back home.

The manager expanded on this last point when Harry eventually ended up back with him. *"I'm afraid we take quite a lot of decisions for our customers. We encourage people to follow the seasons when it comes to fruit and veg – cheaper for all and perfectly safe from a health point of view. If something – say avocadoes – seems expensive, we just don't buy any. Then there can be no argument between those with a bit extra and those without. And most people appreciate a more natural food cycle, like the old days, with proper seasons for fruit. Similarly, we offer a choice between 2 types of toilet paper not 10, 1 kind of champagne – actually usually prosecco – rather than 5, for that special occasion. Old people back East have too much choice and have it rammed down their throats 10 times a day that they are poor relative to others. We soften all those things here and most people really appreciate that."*

Lunch in one of the remaining restaurants was simple but filling (and it cost Harry only 3 Newhome pounds). By 5 pm, he was back at the hotel with his mind rather more on whether he could catch up with Ingrid that evening than on what he had seen. Later, over a drink or two and having concluded that Ingrid was unlikely to be found, Harry did rather better in marshalling his thoughts. As before, and much to his surprise given his initial priors, Harry had to admit that Hetman was doing a good job in convincing him of the merits of Moving On.

Giorgi was around to serve drinks and provide a simple but filling meal. Harry decided early that he needed a quiet night. Perhaps he was already thinking like an older man. He phoned Carl to let him know that he, Harry, was ready to move on the next morning.

15

THE REST HOME

In a dream you are never 80

–Anne Sexton

"The days of our age are three score and ten; and though men be so strong that they come to fourscore years: yet is their strength then but labour and sorrow; so soon passeth it away and we are gone."

–Psalm 90, verse 10

The weather the next morning was still bright and warm. Jeff appeared with the car about 9.30 and said he would be driving Harry up the coast about 10 miles, to a village for the older and more infirm. *"Very pleasant it is too"* commented Jeff. *"Real sea air and views, not like here. But otherwise the same basic structure as Newhome, just more carers and nurses; oh, and better internal security to stop people wandering – too much dementia around to do anything else."*

The car drove out of Newhome, stopping at what was now an exit barrier. And then about 6 miles up the coast. *"Used to be called Padstow, I believe"* said Jeff. *"They had to leave bits on the other side of the water, like Rock, in the private sector – I was told it was too expensive to buy out.*

67

But this town has the advantage of being fairly cut off, so if anyone did go wandering – and I'm sure they do here – they won't get far."

Harry rolled down the window and sniffed the sea air appreciatively. This was more like his idea of English seaside. The perimeter barrier this time was much closer to the town than in the case of Newhome; and only about 4 minutes later, the car was pulling up outside what Harry thought had probably once been the Town Hall.

They were clearly expected, for within a few seconds, a middle-aged woman had come out, walked sharply down the steps and was pulling open Harry's door. She thrust a hand at him the moment he had got out of the car. *"Hello. I'm Agatha the Town Manager. You must be Harry. We've been expecting you."* She turned and marched back up the stairs, through the door. Harry grabbed his rucksack of possessions and chased after her.

Agatha's office turned out to be a functional, rather utilitarian, room just inside the main doors. *"Make yourself at home"* she said *"and I'll explain what I've arranged following the advice I received from the Minister. Coffee or tea?"*

Harry declined politely, saying he had only recently had breakfast. *"Well now"* resumed Agatha. *"Let me tell you a bit about Dun Moving – which is what we call this place. God knows how many bureaucrats it took to come up with that name. But there we are, we're stuck with it, the first inhabitants voted for it – and it's certainly an accurate description for the people here.*

Right, history first. About 3,000 residents, been going 6 years. No-one comes here unless they are over 80, or sick – probably cancer or dementia. So, the pace of life is slow. Much of what action there is revolves round the hospital, which is the only really new building we had to create when we came. Otherwise, the odd pub, day centre and restaurant. And a pattern of living just like the one they will have experienced in Newhome or wherever they came from. From what the Minister said, I was left a bit unclear what we could best do to meet your needs. So, I've arranged for you to visit some of the doctors who run the hospital and get a detailed briefing from them. One of my assistants will come with you, then walk you round the town and feed you. This afternoon I've arranged for a group of residents to talk to you at the main day centre. But, to be honest, half of them won't be too clear what day of the week it is or where they are; so please go easy on them and treat what you get back from them with a firm pinch of salt. Then, finally, back to my house. We don't have the luxury of a hotel or anything like that. So you'll have to make do with my hospitality for the night. Then we can see what you may want to do tomorrow."

Harry had to admit to himself that, as before, Hetman's organisation seemed impeccable. And while, especially here, he could see that Agatha might well have arranged that the people he met were ones who would feed him a pre-agreed line, there was no doubting that the programme covered the main bases for him. And he had to admit that, even if it were possible to convene a genuinely random group of residents to talk to, the last thing he wanted was to deal with a room full of disorientated and maybe sick people. So having them preselected by Agatha was probably the best that could be done in the circumstances.

He left with Mae, one of Agatha's assistants, about 15 minutes later;and they walked together up the hill to the hospital. *"How did you get here?"* he asked her. *"It's been about 3 years now. I volunteered back East when I couldn't find a job I could really settle into. The pay isn't bad, the paid leave is great –I think we'd all go mad here if it weren't. It's not too hard to be patient with people if you know you get 1 week in 4 back East. And Angela's not a bad old stick. With luck in the next couple of years she'll fix me an Assistant Manager job somewhere down here."*

As befitted a building that must have been constructed no more than 6 years ago, the hospital gleamed quietly in the late summer sun. As they pushed through the main doors, Harry immediately smelt the mixture of heat and unknown chemicals – probably mostly disinfectant – that seems to go with hospitals the world over. Mae explained that there were several doctors' surgeries around the town; and a large one in a sector of the town that had been identified for those with dementia. But all serious medical work was done here.

The Consultant in charge, Dr. Garston, was waiting for them up in a plush office on the top floor of the building. Introductions were made, coffee was offered – and this time accepted by Harry – and Mae sat politely out of Harry's line of sight, so that she was as inconspicuous as possible. Dr. Garston seemed at ease and briefly outlined how the medical facilities in the town were organised.

Harry jotted down a few notes and, at the end of what was obviously a speech Garston had made several times before, Harry could see what were the areas he needed to cover in more detail.

"I don't really understand how you can organise a full range of medical facilities in this one set of buildings" Harry began. Garston immediately explained. *"Two things you need to understand. First, we need only facilities for the relatively elderly – not babies, children or young adults. Simplifies things a lot.*

Second, I don't want you to think that we try to offer

services that do more for a patient than you would find in the better hospitals back East. We try to be realistic. We don't perform complex heart surgery – what would be the point really on someone of say 85? Yes, we do provide a full range of chemotherapy for the simpler cancers; but we don't look to prolong life in a bad cancer case beyond where the individual wants to live. We have a cross-check committee system in which independent medical experts help look at an individual case and talk extensively to the individual, to find out what he or she wants to do. And we try and balance the various considerations. We don't prolong life if that comes with pain and suffering. When you know that every case you will be dealing with is elderly then, so long as you frame your own thought processes properly, it's amazing how much one expert can do. Everyone here lives within a mile of the hospital. Hardly anyone misses an appointment – we arrange for patients to be collected from their homes if there is any doubt about their getting here. It all makes life simpler and, I have to say, more efficient."

"Tell me about your staff" said Harry. "All I can say" replied Garston "is thank God for Poles and Filipinos. Getting enough British staff to work here can be difficult. But there are no such problems if you look in the right places abroad. So the Ministry back East do all our recruitment for us; and everyone who comes to work here gets great leave breaks – well, at least the British do – so there's always a trip back East to look forward to and plan for in the near future. Staffing is not one of our great problems."

"So, what are your 'great problems'?" asked Harry. Garston thought for a moment. *"Well, ensuring a steady supply of the right medication can be difficult. Also, our Ministry friends back East don't always understand the importance of our single sex ward policy – which, I have to*

say, our patients strongly support. It isn't straightforward to guess the balance of the sexes and the number of patients so we can't always stick to single sex wards. The dementia section of the town always worries me. It's so hard to know how to strike the right balance there between monitoring and interfering with their freedom. But generally I can honestly say that my problems here have never been as great as those I found when I was running a major unit back East. In particular, no problems with elderly bed-blockers. Everyone who is here is genuinely ill and, as soon as they are well enough to go back into the environment, we can either get them back where they came from or put them into nursing homes which are halfway between hospital and normal life."

Harry could think of no easy way to ask about the mixture of people here or, as he would put it on the basis of what he knew, the preponderance of Party members. He also admitted to himself that he didn't know enough about dementia to be able to ask intelligent questions of Dr. Garston in that area – or about cancer treatment come to that. It seemed time to allow Garston to feel he had achieved whatever it was he had set out to achieve and hope for some insights as he went round.

So, after a desultory wind -down in the conversation, Harry let himself be given a tour of the hospital, and then met up with a couple of medical staff on the ward. From there, it was time for a quick canteen lunch – where the food was at least hot and looked reasonably nutritious – and then on to meet with the preselected group of older residents.

By 4pm Harry had had more than enough. And his notes listed that, indeed by 2pm, he had sent word to Agatha, saying that he was unlikely to want to stay over much into the next day; so could she please see if a flight back East could be laid on from Newquay the next morning. Harry realised –perhaps for the first time explicitly – that he didn't much like the company of visibly sick people; and that old and sick people did even less for him.

All he had concluded from the 4 hours or so he had spent looking around after talking with Garston had been summarised in very brief notes:- hospital looks clean, the wards OK and the staff seemingly pleasant and unstressed;- the doctors make no pretence that they do any significant research into what they treat or that they want to do more than a competent job where their patients suffer as little as possible;- dementia care seems relaxed and patient-friendly. (Harry had for example established that all dementia patients were tagged to indicate their whereabouts if they strayed; but these patients seemed happy and as relaxed as the staff about how they were treated.)- there was no luxury on the wards or elsewhere. But, at the same time, beds and staff looked clean, and equipment seemed in good working order as far as he could tell.

When Harry returned to the Manager's house, where he was to spend the night, he was happy to find that indeed London could airlift him out tomorrow; and that arrangements had already been made to get him to Newquay in good time. As Agatha herself put it succinctly *"They are no doubt as happy in London as Carl and I that we have managed to satisfy your questions in just 3 days. We can get on with our work, of which there is always plenty, and you presumably can have an unexpectedly long and quiet weekend back in London."*

Dinner that night was accompanied by what Agatha

described as the best wine made in Cornwall – a white from the Camel Valley around Newhome. A couple of visitors for dinner had been arranged, one of whom – an Anglican clergyman – Harry found mildly interesting to talk to. But the priest, seemingly like everyone else, had no comment to offer on other towns in the area, having never been posted anywhere except here.

Harry slept well. And, around 11 am the next morning, he quietly toasted himself in a very early g&t as the plane home took off from Newquay.

16

NEXT STEPS

Harry had obviously caught London by surprise, in deciding to come back on Thursday. Simon therefore put up no resistance when Harry contacted him and said he intended to enjoy a long weekend at the hotel. What Simon did do was to warn that he would have to seek instructions from Hetman about the next steps and that Harry could expect a call at the hotel well before Monday morning.

Simon indeed rang on Saturday morning to say that Harry should come to the Interior Ministry before 10 on Monday and be prepared to travel for a few days. He also said that Hetman personally wanted to check up on progress so far; and that Harry should meet Hetman in the main bar of the hotel at 6 that evening. Simon explained *"Hetman will be on his way to a dinner somewhere. But he wants to get a reading from the horse's mouth now to find out how things are going."*

This suited Harry perfectly well. He packed Carol off to the hotel spa for some exotic massage involving hot stones and special rubs. And 6pm sharp saw him nursing a drink in the main bar.

Hetman was a few minutes late and made no apology as he sat himself down next to Harry, who had thought ahead and arranged himself at one end of a long and fortunately people-free bar. So there would be little risk of any conversation being overheard. Maybe the barman didn't know who the new arrival was; but he kept well away until Hetman rapped sharply on the bar and indicated to the barman that he should bring another full glass for Harry and the same for himself. Once these had duly arrived, the barman retreated again and Hetman turned to his companion.

"*I hope your early return to London didn't mean anything went wrong on your little trip*" Hetman said. "*The 2 village managers both reported back that you seemed happy enough and indeed that your requests had been very reasonable and easy to meet. Similarly Claire and John both reported that they thought they had met your briefing needs pretty well. I want to know how you think things are going. And I need to explain a few background facts before your jaunt to Europe next week. We have a maximum of an hour but I'm sure you can get back to your girl-friend well before that if things are indeed going well.*"

Harry had thought hard about what he would say to Hetman about progress so far. "*Well, I can confirm that the arrangements so far have been faultless and that the briefings and the trip have been very useful. Thank you for all of that, especially given how little time you had. Now, I do have some remaining reservations – the key one of which I'll come back to – but in general, you'll be pleased to know that I can see a lot of sense in what you are contemplating, whether one looks at the issues from the point of view of those who might be Moving On or from your viewpoint in government. And that already allows for the fact that you wouldn't be human if what you have set up for me hadn't been arranged to put the best gloss on things for you.*"

Hetman swivelled a little on his bar stool and re-crossed his legs to get comfortable. *"Well, that's encouraging. What's your 'key reservation'?"* Harry had also thought carefully about what he would say here. *"Not to beat about the bush, it may just have been chance; but what I saw down in the South-West seemed primarily to have benefitted elderly denizens of the PDP. I shall want to go and find some more ordinary folk, who have Moved On, to check that they have a similarly upbeat tale to tell. Otherwise, so far so good. Especially for the really elderly."*

Hetman seemed happy enough with this and, after a brief pause switched the subject. *"That's good news and I'll give some thought to how we might be able to reassure you this is not just a PDP retirement plan. Let's talk now about the next week, in Europe which is going to be a rather different kettle of fish. My writ of course doesn't run there like it does here, so I have had to entrust your care there to people I largely don't know and don't trust. I've also had to finesse, as best I can, the fact that there are all sorts of shades of treatment for elderly people in Europe and different ones again in places like the US. For now – and I don't rule out future short trips for you – I've arranged for a week's programme to be organised for you in Paris and provided by a mixed group of Europeans. There's also an American woman, Lise, in the group who has a French mother and who has agreed to act as your main interpreter and intermediary. They understand you need to operate in English so far as possible, so that shouldn't be much of a problem. I should hasten to add that Lise is someone I would never employ here in London; so I think you will see quite readily that I haven't set her up to show you what I want.*

I'm pretty sure there'll be a lot more talking and less action than you've had in the last couple of weeks; and you will also find some weird groups I've barely heard of. For example, Lise was on this week about your meeting at least one transhumanist – good, I didn't know what that was and I can see by your face you are equally foxed. Anyway, we'll just have to see how you get on and, remember, Tara will be around to hold your hand (as it were); and she can always get back to me if things get sticky.

What I do need to do now, though, is just to take you through something that you almost certainly know about as well as I do; but it needs to be done. And that is to explain about how we have handled 'information flow' for you. Now, I know you understand very well the limits that have been in force in this country for many years about the dissemination of information on the web and about access to foreign sources of information. I know the restrictions seemed wholly bad news to people like you at the time; but I've always thought our crashing out of Europe, the plague and the CIA/Red China cyberwar of 2025 were all actually quite helpful in their way. Certainly, they enabled my predecessors to set boundaries on internet access and information gathering that have helped to keep this country relatively free from unwholesome foreign influence.

Now I can well imagine (and won't ask about) the fact that you and your paper probably are familiar with all sorts of ways to get round the firewalls and restraints, to access some of that foreign information. That's one of the safety valves we allow in the system. But, even so, I suspect you will still be knocked back by the chaotic free-for-all that passes for information flow somewhere like Paris.

I did wonder whether I shouldn't just authorise you to be able to access anything on the world-wide web, so that you could do your own trawling for information before you meet these people. In the end, I decided not to do that.

My own remit only runs so far; and, for obvious reasons, there are lots of people who work for us who need access to foreign sources of information more than you do. Also, as everywhere else – and this is one good reason why we retain all the limitations here – you have endless 'fake news' out there. You wouldn't know what was probably true and what wasn't. I thought – and you may disagree – that you would do better if I set up a dialogue for you in person with the people you're going to meet. No priors, other than what you now know about what happens in England.

To start with, I've arranged that you and Tara stay in Paris for a week; and I know she is determined to fit a bit of sightseeing into that programme. Let's take stock at the end of that. I don't rule out your making other foreign trips. Just keep in mind the fact that I am now only 2 weeks away from the launch of our Moving On proposals. And by then, we need you to have substantial initial material written, to help direct public debate from Day 1. In other words, there isn't much time."

17

TO PARIS

"They order, said I, this matter better in France."
–Laurence Sterne A Sentimental Journey

"Good Americans, when they die, go to Paris"
–Oliver Wendell Holmes in The Autocrat of the breakfast table.

Despite Hetman's urgency, Harry felt relaxed as he arrived at the Interior Ministry on Monday morning, wheeling a small suitcase, rather than the bag of last week. He hadn't been to Paris since he was a young man. Indeed, he hadn't been anywhere in Europe since then, if one did not count the fortnights in the Costa del Sol that the British Government had retained and paid well for since the split from Europe. Like most professionals, Harry had been eligible for many years to have 2 weeks in the sun every second year in Spain, in areas ringed off – now he thought about it – rather like Newhome that he had visited last week. Though language and cash were the barriers in Spain, not a physical restraint like at Newhome. Harry didn't go much for 'culture'; but even he had always found these periods of enforced sun-lounging left him depressed and out of sorts when

80

he had got home. That's why Hetman's offer had been so attractive.

Simon was waiting for him and took him quickly through the travel documents he would need for the trip. *"There's a few hundred euro as well, though Tara will have most of what you need. And Harry"* Simon stopped and looked like he actually might be going to hug Harry *"I can't tell you how pleased I am that Hetman is happy with where you are and what you have been doing. It means so much to Tara and me. And I know she'll be taking good care of you over the next few days to make sure nothing goes wrong. She'll meet you at the airport. Bonne chance, Harry – enjoy your time away."*

There was little more to say on either side, so Harry soon found himself back in an official car heading (again) to Northolt. There he discovered that he and Tara were actually the only passengers on what was obviously a small military plane equipped for a minimal number of passengers. Not for the first time, he marvelled at the levers Hetman seemed able to pull.

He boarded, to find Tara already sitting in one of the front seats. She seemed pleased to see him but made no effort to do more than acknowledge the perfunctory kiss on the cheek that he offered her. *"It must be months since I've seen you"* she said. *"But I can't think of a better way to get together again than a week in Paris. And just to put your mind at rest, Harry. Whatever Simon said to you, I have no interest in your tedious enquiries. This is the deal I'm offering. You do your work, I sight-see and shop. And we both swear blind when we get back that I was around with you nearly all the time. I am here really only to see you are looked after and that you enjoy yourself as far as your schedule permits. I have no real part in what you're doing for Simon. I just want to bring you back in one piece, after a good week away, so you can get on with whatever Hetman and you are cooking up."*

With that, she turned back to look out of the window seat her early arrival had made possible. As Harry reflected, she was probably just as happy as he was to be spending a week away in Paris; and he could see the attractions for her of avoiding most of the work schedule, whatever that was going to be.

The journey was uneventful; and the Immigration officials at the small military airport they landed at near Paris were non-existent. Harry and Tara were introduced to a young man who spoke flawless English (only his lack of any real accent and the oddly mechanical way he sometimes spoke gave clues that he was not British). And, by mid-afternoon (allowing for the local hour advancement of the clocks they had been warned about), they were ensconced in a 5-star hotel near the Champs-Elysee. Tara nearly purred with delight when the destination became clear; and again when they were shown to 2 adjacent luxury rooms at the top of the building, with magnificent views over central Paris.

There was also a note for Harry saying that Lise and one of her colleagues would meet them in the bar on the first floor at 6pm, to discuss the work programme they had fixed up. Harry knew that unpunctuality was not one of Tara's faults, so it was no surprise when he was able to pick her up from her room at 5 minutes to 6 and take the lift down to the First Floor.

The bar already had a smattering of people sitting in it; but Harry, as he quickly scanned the room, could only see one couple who might obviously be Lise and her companion. The rest were men presumably winding down from their day. Lise, if it was her, glanced at him and Harry felt as though he had been kicked in the solar plexus. Certainly, he was a ladies' man and assuredly he liked a pretty face. But this woman, probably in her mid-30s and very obviously expensively dressed, was something special. Dark hair in ringlets falling to shoulder length. A beautifully proportioned face with what Harry could see from 5 yards away was dominated by 2 bewitching and smiling blue eyes. As she and her companion rose, with Harry mouthing a prayer to himself that this was indeed Lise, he could also see she had a lithe svelte figure, with long shapely legs.

It might have been very embarrassing for Harry had this not been Lise – Harry was sure his face had already betrayed to any keen onlooker how much he had been struck by her. Fortunately, she almost immediately moved towards Tara and Harry, held out a hand to him and said *"I'm Lise, this is Jochen. And I can see from my briefing – which did include photos I hasten to add – that you are Harry and Tara. Welcome to Paris and to our few days together.* She smiled at Harry as she said this; and any remaining self-restraint Harry felt melted in the light of that smile.

Jochen turned out to be a rather taciturn German but his English was excellent and he had obviously decided not to butt in at any point unless he had something relevant to say. Lise, for her part, had a beautiful lilting French accent to her perfect English – though Harry, even in his present state of mind, did notice that she occasionally used phrases that weren't really English but – he presumed – were perhaps the result of her half-American parentage.

Tara and Harry were immediately made to feel welcome. A bottle of Veuve Clicquot and 4 glasses appeared as if by magic (Harry had no eyes for the barman who quickly and unobtrusively brought them, having obviously received his orders in advance). A pleasant drink turned, after about half an hour, into dinner at the restaurant next to the bar. And, by the end of that, about 2 hours later, Harry was feeling so good that he was surprised to see that his feet were still firmly on the floor, even if his mind was contemplating something quite different.

Lise controlled the proceedings throughout. At the outset, she was obviously unsure of the relation between Harry and Tara so she made a point early on of talking mostly to Tara in very friendly fashion. Lise quickly established that Tara was primarily interested in the Eiffel Tower, Notre Dame, the Louvre, the Musee D'Orsay and shopping. So, even before they rose to move to the restaurant, the 2 women were focused on just what order Tara might do things in and how Lise's colleagues might be able to help.

It was only over dinner that the talk turned to what Harry was there for. Lise smiled across the table at him, over the amuse bouche, and said *"Well, Harry. We have taken a small conference room here at the hotel for the week and, as far as possible, we thought we'd bring people to you rather than vice versa, to maximise your effective time. You'll meet a number of my colleagues over the week. Jochen here will talk about care of the elderly around Europe, mostly focusing on Germany, the Netherlands and Scandinavia. I will cover North America and in between we have a few short visits for you to a nearby hospital, a hospice and what I suppose you would call a retirement home. Oh, and just to make that all seem a bit more palatable, we'll throw in the occasional oddball, like the gentleman who is convinced that people like him will eventually live for ever.*

Insofar as I've ever understood what he's on about, he thinks either that eventually it will be possible to reverse ageing or – perhaps 'and' – merge his sentience with the Artificial Intelligence of a computer. That would enable something that is 'him' to live on for ever in a machine. We call such people transhumanists, I don't know you really have an English word for them seeing – as I understand it – England opted out of the computer era round about the time AI was coming in."

It was nearly 10pm before the party broke up. Lise said, smiling – now smiling almost all the time at Harry – *"We have a busy day tomorrow, starting let's say 9.30 in the Monet Conference room on the second floor which is what we've booked for the week."* Her smile transferred itself to Tara. *"And for you, I suggest that Sylvain – a Parisian who I think you will find delightful – should meet you at Reception at 10. The 2 of you can start on a tour of Paris; he will make a first rate guide. I will brief him tonight. Oh, by the way, don't worry about the costs of what we're doing. The little Institute I am attached to has a very generous donor behind it. I believe he was originally English; he was certainly happy to say he would cover all our costs."*

Tara and Harry rode up to their rooms in silence. Outside her door, Tara looked Harry carefully in the face and said *"Now Harry. I can see from your behaviour tonight that we are going to have to be careful that Lise, whatever her name is, doesn't exercise undue influence over you in the next few days. If you can't keep your prick in your trousers then we'd better make sure I spend the nights with you. I shouldn't mind"* – she reached up and stroked his face – *"you're very attractive in spite of being as old as Methuselah. And a little 'interaction' between us might anyway be a good way of making sure that you don't spill the beans back home to Simon about how we've spent our time here. Of course, if Sylvain turns out to be a really good guide – the kind I want 24/7 – I may not have time for you too. But I shall be keeping a close eye; and I shall want to hear every day how the programme is going."* With that, she smiled again fleetingly, opened her room with her plastic card key, and left Harry to his own very mixed thoughts in the corridor.

18

IF I WERE A RICH MAN…

"It [France] is a land of milk and honey, the best milk and the most perfumed honey, where all the good things of the earth overflow and are cooked to perfection."
–William Bolitho *Camera Obscura*

Harry had never had much chance to appreciate the strengths (and weaknesses) of a good continental breakfast, of the kind he enjoyed the following morning. But he did appreciate the strength of the coffee; and the taste and smell of the croissants and accompanying jam brought back some vague but happy memories from his childhood.

Tara was with him but very much in her own world as she thought about what the first day's sightseeing might bring. At the end of breakfast, she murmured to Harry *"Good luck. I'll see you tonight, maybe for dinner. Behave yourself but have as good a day as I intend to. And remember the deal."*

Just before 9.30, Harry pushed through the large heavy doors of the Monet Conference Room. Back in London, the haphazard timekeeping of most continentals was a standing joke. But here, perhaps because Jochen was

German and Lise American, Harry was not surprised to find that the doors swung open to a sizeable room that was already occupied by 5 or 6 people. Lise rose on his arrival and came over to make the introductions for the rest of her party. As she had promised, it was clear that – with this group at least – Harry's lack of another European language was not going to be a problem.

Within 5 minutes, Lise had made the introductions and got people sat round the large oval table that took up the centre of the room. Harry was relieved to find that he was not isolated, so that it didn't look like it was 1 against 6. He had also had some reassurance immediately from the first round of introductions that he was dealing with a mixture of professional people – an economist, a sociologist, and at least one medical doctor among them, all of whom might be expected to help Harry wrestle with what he accepted was an impossibly large and complex agenda.

They all sat. At Lise's invitation, Harry spoke briefly about why he was there. As with Ingrid just those few days earlier, he was circumspect in what he said but as open as he felt he could be; the truth but not all the truth. *"I'm here"* Harry said *"because the English Government is reviewing the way it treats the elderly; I am helping with that review; and, while we think that much of the rest of the world is pursuing goals very different from our own, we did think that it would be good to hear at first-hand how other countries are tackling the same issues that we face. So, I am here for a very preliminary introduction to what is done elsewhere and why.*

Please call me Harry; and let's please cut the formalities to a minimum – there just won't be time otherwise. Also, please understand that I know that there is a very strict limit to what you could tell me or what I could absorb in the few days I have here. So, to focus on what I need to hear, I have taken the liberty of jotting down the main issues I'd like us to concentrate on. These are as follows.." and Harry produced about 10 copies of a piece of paper he had had typed out in London, handing them on to Lise, who quickly passed them round the table. *"In no particular order:*

Are people over 65 a net economic burden to society and, if so, how is that burden shared? Or should that figure be 75?

Do your countries encourage older people to live in the community or do you find ways of separating them out and bringing them together?

What are the main issues over the care of older people? For example, adequate resources – money and human?

How is the picture going to change over time? Developments actual or prospective in medical treatment? Is what you do sustainable in the longer-term? What priorities would you urge us to take into account? What are the main problems we should look out for?

There was a short silence when Harry finished speaking and the others in the room looked at each other a little uneasily. Lise was the first to respond.

"Well, Harry, that's helpful though I guess it would have helped us even more to have had these questions in advance. Fortunately, they are not too far away from what I guessed you wanted, based on what London told us. So, I'm sure we can get to the substance of what you want. What we do need to do now, though, is to look at the rough outline of the week we had planned for you against your specific issues; and then work out how best to use our time. I had already told my colleagues that we should keep formal presentations to a minimum; and it was always obvious that you wouldn't

have time (nor want much) to see how older people actually live in and around Paris. So, it's bound to be mostly dialogue, not action."

Lise paused and looked round at her colleagues. *"What I suggest happens now is that we go into conclave and rework our schedules in the light of what you have told us. Give us, say, an hour – we Americans at least are at our best against deadlines"* she smiled at Harry, for the first time that morning, to take any implicit criticism out of her words. *"The coffee next door is excellent I believe. Bear with us and we'll invite you back just as soon as we can."*

It actually took nearer 90 minutes for the door of the Monet Room to open and for Harry to be invited back. Again, Lise did all the talking from her side; it was already obvious that she was much more than just the translator and organiser of the event. The others clearly relied on her to lead them.

"OK, Harry. We've salvaged what we can of the work we'd already prepared and we've agreed how to regroup the rest. You have just 3 ½ days at most, so I suggest that we start on the new format. If it's acceptable to you, let's hear from you before lunch what's bugging the English Government and what problems you think you have to fix. After lunch – and no meeting in Paris is worth having without giving serious time in the middle of the day to good food – we'll take the first of your questions and use that for a round table debate. Then, over the week, we'll do the same to the other questions.

In between times, I'll organise a few – and I mean a couple of – visits from people who can speak with closer knowledge of some of the topics. So, for example, we'll get the Head of the European Pharmaceutical Agency (which as you may know is based here in Paris) to talk about medical innovations. We've also had a couple of outsiders who have heard about your coming and insist on meeting you. The people in that category we won't be able to say 'no' to are certainly the Head of the 'Dying in Dignity' League and the leader of the main transhumanist body in the US, who has already flown over from Los Angeles to bend your ear."

Jochen then spoke, for the first time in the meeting. *"I am reluctant to try and speak for everyone on this side of the table."* If Lise didn't, he certainly did seem to view the meeting as Harry against the rest. *"But I must be frank. What little we know of what goes on England suggests that your Government is what we regard as profoundly undemocratic and uncaring. All of us on this side of the table, however, regard ourselves as the exact reverse; and try as hard as we can, much of what we say to you will undoubtedly be flavoured with a humanist and caring touch that I suspect would go down badly where you come from. It won't be aimed at you as such; I believe that the Americans have a saying "it's not personal, it's business". And that is what it will be for us."*

Harry thanked Lise and Jochen and looked quickly round the table. *"That all sounds like a very sensible use of time. And I can assure you that, from my long years as a journalist, I have developed quite a thick skin. I doubt if anything you could say about England or our Government will do more than bounce off that skin. Also I say again that my visit may just be the start of a longer relationship"* –Harry couldn't stop his glance passing briefly over Lise as he said this – *"So let's regard these few days as the chance for everyone to set out their respective stalls and not as likely to lead to the resolution of what I'm sure – when you've heard what I have to say – are real and major problems."*

Between 11.30 and lunch, Harry briefly recapitulated

for them the kind of issues that Hetman had set out at the start of his work, what he – Harry – had been doing in the last few weeks and why he had framed the 4 questions for them as he had. As he did so, a tiny part of Harry's mind sat back and patted himself on the back. Like the good journalist he thought he was, Harry had absorbed a huge amount of material since first meeting Hetman; and, Harry hoped, an outsider listening to him now could not fail to be impressed by his grip on the major issues.

For much of the time, the others listened quietly. But when there were questions or discussion, Harry was quickly reassured that most, if not all of those present, had such a good grasp of working English that one of his initial fears – that there would be endless linguistic problems – was unfounded. Just twice Lise intervened to say a few sentences in what Harry knew was French and, once in what he thought was German, to elucidate some point he had made. During the course of these exchanges, Harry was again reassured, this time by the fact that Lise at least seemed to have a close and current knowledge of how politics and social events in England had developed over the last 2 decades. The others might not like the line of some of Harry's questioning over the next few days, he thought; or they might well be totally out of sympathy with the social and political views that underlay his questions. But, if he could not do it himself, Harry was at least now fairly confident that Lise would be a help in putting it all in a context, potentially at least, to which they might be able to relate.

19

I'VE NEVER MET A TRANSHUMANIST BEFORE

"May you live as long as you want And never want as long as you live"

–A traditional benediction.

The next 3 days were a blur for Harry. Not since his college days had he been talked to so intensively; and, because he was alone, he had no choice but to be fully engaged for every minute of each discussion.

The routine that Lise had suggested worked out pretty well. She kept a close rein on how time was spent and regularly seemed to be steering those involved gently (sometimes not so gently) back to the main subjects. For the 'other side', Lise, Jochen and an Italian girl called Vittoria did most of the talking. A coffee break was allowed around 11 and again at 4; an excellent lunch was served each day in an adjacent room at 1pm promptly. And, each evening, Lise arranged a small dinner at the hotel with Harry, herself and at most 2 other attendees. (It had become obvious, from a message on Tuesday from Tara, that she would have other plans for dinner each night.) These dinners were deliberately focused on subjects that were related to the main topics but which did not fall naturally into the sessions. Thus it was here that Harry one night had to endure something of a monologue from a representative of *Dying in Dignity* about when an elderly or sick person should be allowed to arrange or speed their own death.

On another evening, the dinner was attended by 2 delightful but – to him – odd Americans. They talked at length about their aim to live for ever. This turned out to require further medical advance to roll back the ageing process or developments in Artificial Intelligence (AI) that would make it possible for individuals to transfer some version of their consciousness to a machine that would continue after their own deaths.

The dinners finished around 9pm each evening. Harry would then scribble notes up about his experiences that day; and around 11pm each night, he had to close his day with a nightcap with Tara, so that she could check he was still on the straight and narrow.

There were good points about this regime. Tara was obviously enjoying her days – and it turned out quickly her evenings -with Sylvain. That had the advantage for Harry that Tara was fairly business-like when they met up last thing; and she made no more allusions to keeping an eye on Harry at night. It was also a regime that allowed a huge range of topics to be covered, albeit – he accepted often very superficially – in a very limited time. But Harry inevitably found the process immensely draining; and, even more important for him as the week progressed, he was never alone with Lise for more than a couple of minutes. She seemed, to his mind, always to ensure that there was at least one other member of her 'team' (as he came to think of them) with them.

Certainly, he never had long enough with her alone to start to form a real relationship with her. That worried him increasingly. The more he saw of her the more he became convinced that here was a woman that he could come to love and cherish in a way that he hadn't done with any woman since his teenage years. It wasn't just for the obvious reasons. She was beautiful, yes. She dressed well and alluringly but demurely, yes. (Harry was not familiar with modern French perfume but was conscious always of her scent; and went to sleep each evening imagining it was on the pillow next to him.) But what he liked to think most important, she was a highly intelligent and engaging woman, the like of which – despite his long involvement with many layers of British society – he had rarely come across before. Before he left Paris, he just had to find a way to spend time with her alone, to see if she could reciprocate any of his feelings.

That chance came unexpectedly on Friday afternoon, after the usual afternoon coffee break. Lise had managed, before coffee, to bring the topic they had been discussing – the likely effect of prospective medical advances on life expectancy and on improving the quality of life – to a fairly natural conclusion. Now, as they resumed, Lise said *"Well, I think we have to draw a line somewhere. I'd like to thank all my companions for their huge contribution over the last 4 days. I think, Harry, it's time for you to say adieu to them. If I may be so bold, I'd like to invite you to a private supper this evening, just you and me. I want to get your first reflections and decide if there is more to be done."*

Harry couldn't have hoped for anything better. *"Fine with me. Shall we say that we meet in the bar here at 6? I'll use the time between now and then to summarise my main thoughts." "I suggest that we actually meet in the Café d'Or*

95

which is nearby" she replied. *"It's my favourite restaurant in this part of Paris; and I think you've earned a culinary treat. The desk here can give you directions very easily. Say 7 pm; that's way too early for a Frenchman to eat but we can make an exception for you."*

20

AN EVENING TOGETHER

Harry had less than 3 hours and he knew that he would need most of that to marshal his thoughts. He had to make the right impression on her and also find a way to keep the link between them active. He also realised that he still had very little idea quite why Lise and her colleagues had spent so much time and effort on him, when they hadn't really known what he was doing. If he could work out *her* possible interest, he might be able to frame his own thoughts in a way that made it more likely she would want to keep in touch. He had no illusions how difficult it would be to keep any proper line of communication open with her once he was back in England. But he knew he had to try and that this was the best way to do it.

Very quickly early in the week, he had established to his own satisfaction that Lise, Jochen and the others all thought along completely different lines from those he had always experienced in England. So he had to start from that reality. The key difference he had eventually concluded was that their philosophy of life was quite different to the one he was used to. The prime difference was that they still had faith that technology could solve most problems and therefore could afford the means to accommodate the needs of the elderly.

Harry had no idea of the numbers – he reflected that the English press rarely carried statistics about how the home economy compared with that of overseas rivals. But ever since he had arrived in Paris, his senses had been almost overwhelmed by evidence that real income levels here were far higher than in England. Everywhere – whether it was in the almost uniform use of self-driving cars or what he had heard about the ubiquitous employment of robots – he had seen just how different economic resource allocation problems looked to these people. After all, if your cake was say 50% bigger than that of the person next to you, it wasn't so hard to work out how an extra 5% for one group like the aged could be found without too much trouble.

That realisation had involved some challenges for him. The first time he had got into a car – from the airport – that then started into motion without an apparent driver, he had felt a desperate urge to jump out before there had to be the inevitable crash. It had taken the combined efforts of Tara (who had apparently seen self-drive cars before) and the man who had picked them up to calm him enough for the journey to continue.

Likewise, his first introduction to what the French obviously regarded as normal IT use. The second time he had walked into the hotel bar, the screen behind the bar had sprung eerily into life and a voice had not only welcomed him by name but asked him whether he would like the gin and tonic he had had the first time. One of his hosts had assured him not only that this was normal but had also reeled off examples from 'everyday life' where the French – and apparently most of the rest of Europe

– had got used to using records of past behaviour and preferences to cut the work that the remaining humans in the chain still had to do. In this first case, for Harry, this had led to the barman appearing with his g&t shortly after he had stammered out to the screen (which, to make matters worse had spoken to him in English) that, yes, he would like that drink again.

Harry had felt less but considerable shock the only time on the trip when he had seen first-hand the mass use of robots for the elderly. This experience – in the nearby dementia home that Lise had managed to fit into the timetable on Wednesday – had been cathartic. As the doctor who showed them round had put it, *"These bots work 24/7. They are brilliant at doing simple repetitive tasks – and that includes talking to someone who asks them the same question twenty times an hour because their memory span is 20 seconds. We use human labour still for the more complex tasks, though I suspect within 10 years we will have enabled these machines to do much more. And, if you could ask one of the dementia sufferers which they preferred – 30 minutes talking time a day with a human or the chance to talk almost endlessly with a robot – the answer would be pretty obvious!"*

As with the case of the bar IT, Harry was then supplied by one of Lise's companions with numerous examples of where in the health service information storage and artificial intelligence had been used to stretch the use of human skills (and the cost) much further than before.

One evening, Harry had dared to raise the subject with Tara, thinking that on her tourist excursions she must have seen some other practical examples of what to him was science-fiction IT. It turned out then that, because of Simon's position, Tara had actually managed a number of trips over the years around Europe and was far less fazed about these developments – because they were not new to her – than Harry had been. Harry had very nearly ruined their relationship at that point by asking whether Sylvain's charms had been displaced by computer in any way; but he had had the sense to bite back on the comment as it rose unbidden to his lips.

21

DINNER

"Better is a dinner of herbs where love is, than a stalled ox and hatred therewith."

–Proverbs 17

Harry found his way to the restaurant without difficulty; and, as Lise had forewarned him, there were only a smattering of tables occupied. She was seated, waiting for him with what looked to Harry like a pastis in front of her. (That was one of the many new tastes he had sampled in the last few days – he knew French cooking had always had a good reputation but he had regularly been surprised by how good the food and drink had been.)

"I'm glad we have made time for this" she said. *"I think I know enough of your food and wine tastes to be able to pick for you, if you are not too macho to have a woman choose your food; so shall I order for us both and then we can talk?"* Harry assented though he could never before remember being so passive at a table. Within 5 minutes, a dry white wine for him had appeared; and it was obvious from the corner of the restaurant that Lise had chosen for their table –and the limited number of diners – that their conversation could be private.

"Harry, we have very little time tonight. And we shall

have to get to know each other – and trust each other – unbelievably quickly, if this is to develop as I would like.

First, let me congratulate you on your performance in the last few days. Although you are obviously new to all the medical and other jargon, you clearly have developed in a short space of time a real understanding of what elderly people are like and what they need. When I was first approached to host these few days, I have to admit that I thought it would just be for form, a charade I think you might call it. But in reality, whatever the longer-term aim of what you are doing, you really have come across as someone who wants to search for truth and find viable solutions to real-world problems. I have to admit I have quite come to like you despite the fact that I know little or nothing about the real you. Now, let's hear how you think these few days have gone and what you think may happen next."

Harry felt his face reddening and he looked down out at the table. How could a man of his age and experience feel like a 16 year-old schoolboy with his first possible date? But that is how he felt. And now it was probably make or break time for him, so far as she was concerned.

"Well" he said. *"I hardly know where to begin. I can tell you that, a few weeks ago, I was approached by a senior member of the English Government and asked to review the current state of elderly people in England. The idea was that, as a journalist with what even I would admit is a store of 'street cred' with the public, my views could help influence public opinion. This Government man has major plans for reforming the treatment of old age in England. I agreed to explore what is presently happening and comment on some of the ideas he wants to introduce. With no strings attached as to what I would conclude.*

In the process, I insisted – partly for my own pleasure I

must admit – that I wanted to spend a little time finding out how our issues with the elderly were being dealt with abroad. You can have little idea how irksome are the constraints in England on travelling abroad. Indeed, I only realised how great a loss that is with this trip. But it's what is the norm now in England; and, if anyone ever goes anywhere other than the common 2 weeks in Spain, then they don't talk about it for fear of feeling out of place.

Anyway, this venture for the Government allowed me to negotiate just a few days here – a little holiday really; there was no chance of them agreeing to my going to the US. And that, quite by chance, has led me to be spending these few days with you. These days have been very special for me, purely for personal reasons. If I'm honest" and here Harry looked up, straight into her beautiful blue eyes which were focused fully on him, as though weighing every word he said. *"I never thought it would bring me into touch with someone like you. Someone who – just by their presence – could make me feel 25 again and a free spirit floating in the air above a mass of human and largely minor concerns. Thank you for that from the bottom of my heart.*

I have to admit that these few days have been a shock in another direction too. I knew that England's development path had diverged from what was happening in what we used to call 'the rest of the Western World'. But I had no idea that technology had moved on so much nor that the standard of living here had risen so much.

What that has led me to conclude is that perhaps we are asking the wrong questions in England. We shouldn't be asking how much we can afford to pay for the elderly and how can we reduce those costs? We should instead be asking why are we not richer and better able to afford the cost of the elderly? In particular, why are we so reluctant to adopt new technology which could both raise our standard of living and directly ease the burden of caring for the elderly?

*Don't get me wrong. I don't even begin to think that things here are perfect. Heaven knows what political problems you actually have. You **do** have exactly the same social and psychological problems that we see. I've identified a lot of these and there must be here a growing number of old people, too many of whom are being kept alive without enough regard perhaps to what good it will do them. You haven't cracked some of the worst problems, notably the onset of dementia. And you clearly have an 'interesting' fringe like those transhumanists, alive and well. I couldn't believe what I was hearing that evening. One seemed to think that eventually technology would roll back death for decades or for ever. The other thought that eventually our human identity could be transferred to machines, enabling the individual psyche to live on for ever. That all sounded crazy to me. People like that get no airspace in England, I can tell you.*

But I was impressed by the fact that all this care seemed to be available to poor as well as rich (though I know which I want to be when I get old). So, I'm left with the need to think about whether and how I can change the nature of the debate back in England. And I'm also – much more pressingly for me- left wondering how can I see more of you, how can we start some meaningful relationship; if that was ever something you would consider."

Harry hadn't meant this last thought to spill out but, equally, he had not tried hard to stop it. Either he spoke now or within 24 hours he would be back in his old constrained world and any possible link with Lise would be gone for ever.

There was silence. Eventually, Lise –looking across at

him while stirring her spoon round a now empty plate that had contained a delicious crepe – replied. *"I could see that you found me attractive; that happens so often that I've become almost immune to it. And to be absolutely level with you, I have no idea whether I would find you seriously interesting if we got to know each other better. 'Maybe' is all I can say at this stage though if it helps I can at least say that I am, how you would say, unattached at present. There is also a lot you don't and can't know about me and that might change how you see me when you find out.*

*Let me be perfectly frank with you. Had you not turned up here this week and not shown yourself to be such a decent human being, I would just have wanted to get to the end of the week and pack you back to England. But I am doing something soon in your country that you just might be able to help me with. You will have to take a lot on trust from me. But I have an idea that you could help me and it would at least mean we kept closely in touch, at least for now, as that seems to be what you want. And, I think I can promise you that, when you discover what I'm really trying to do, you **will** want to help me. If you have the courage to publish, you could also get the scoop of a lifetime."*

She paused but only briefly. *"What I shall ask of you will expose you to perhaps a little danger. And I will not be able to tell you much about what I am really doing until we get to the moment where I hope all can be revealed. IF you are willing to contemplate that, then we must start immediately to set up a plausible story.*

A little more detail. I shall want you to accompany me somewhere in England in about 10 days. To someone looking from the outside, you would only do that if you and I were 'an item'. So, the first step, which I'm sure you won't object to, is that you take me back now to your hotel bedroom, making clear to anyone we come across that you and I have had a great evening together. We'll spend the night in your room though I'm afraid that won't go further – at this stage anyway – than shared sleeping arrangements. And, by the time you leave tomorrow to go back to England you will know more what it is I need you to do. It will then be up to you as to whether you follow through. But I can promise that, this way, you will see me again very soon – that I shall be grateful for what you can do for me; and, as I say, you may – on top of that – have the scoop of your life."

Harry said, rather indistinctly, that this would be OK by him, he would happily be involved. Lise called for and paid the bill and they then walked the 7 minutes or so back to Harry's hotel. Harry held her closely to him as they walked and thought it wouldn't stretch things too far if he kissed her a couple of times –allegro, with vigour, as his old music teacher had said; once for the benefit of the maitre-d of the restaurant and once again for the hotel desk staff when they got back to the hotel. Lise entered into the spirit once Harry had murmured to her what he proposed and why. And luck was with them. Harry had feared that they would bump into Tara outside his room. But mercifully that was avoided. Harry and Lise slipped into his room; and Harry could breathe again.

Lise slipped the bag on her shoulder onto the bed; and in a very business-like manner, she delved and brought out a bag of what were obviously overnight personal items – Harry could see a toothbrush and a nightdress ; Lise took these things with her into the bathroom.

About 10 minutes later she reappeared wearing an attractive but not revealing nightdress and walking in a little cloud – it seemed to Harry – of immensely desirable fragrance. What a difference, he thought, to the last time a woman had been in his bedroom – Ingrid nearly 2 weeks ago. Lise laughed softly as Harry stood up and she could see his face. *"Poor Harry. I don't suppose you're the kind of man who at this time of night says goodnight to a girl and puts a pillow in the bed between them. Just as well that your bed is large, otherwise I'm afraid it would have been the floor or a settee for you. But it could be worse"* and here she came up to him, wrapped her arms around him, and of her own volition kissed him long and hard. Eventually she backed away and ran her hands down the side of her nightdress. *"Now, let's get that pillow into place. You will be able to go to sleep with my perfume in your nostrils. I hope that at least makes for sweet dreams."*

22

BACK TO LONDON

The next morning, they took breakfast in the hotel room. Lise said she needed to talk further with him and Harry was anxious to keep Lise away from Tara. Whoever they had to get to believe that Harry and Lise were now together, Harry could see no way that would be helped by Tara getting to know.

Lise was quite talkative by comparison with the night before, especially after the first strong coffee and delicious still warm croissant. *"Harry. I've been thinking over what exactly I can tell you about my planned visit to England. I and one of my team will arrive in London –it's planned for about 10 days' time. We have a little business there, about which the English authorities will doubtless have made enquiries to check they are prepared to let us in; that is how England is these days. Then I need to get out of London for a couple of days and go down to your West Country. I will be able to tell you why when we get to that point.*

So, I suggest that I come to wherever it is you live, on my second evening in London. Please write the address down now. By the time I come, you will have arranged to take me down to Cornwall, hiring a car, so we can spend a couple of days together. It will need to be to a hotel near Rock or one of the wealthier places down there that is still in private hands.

On the second day there, you and I will drive down to the South Cornwall Coast. There is a lovely open-air theatre down there called The Minack whIch I believe still functions. Their season closes at the end of this month but I think you'll easily be able to get 2 tickets to whatever they have on for the day in question. That way, if anyone is monitoring what I am doing – and you know how sensitive your Government is to foreign nationals like me even being in your country – it won't be me organising these things. Hopefully, with your involvement, we will be able to slip off their radar; all I need are 2 days. I promise I will explain more once we are out of London."

"How will we communicate to plan all this?" asked Harry. "Well, I shall have your address. And here" she produced a small electronic device not much bigger than a watch, out of the bag lying on her side of the bed *"here is a small and simple bit of kit. This will only receive messages not send them. But I will tell you through this as soon as I have the exact dates for our visit to London. You will then know exactly when to book the car and a hotel down in Cornwall. Plus the date for the theatre tickets. You can leave all the rest to me. But I assume, with your standing and contacts, it won't exactly be hard for you to book a car, a hotel for 2 nights and get whatever clearance you need to drive round the country with me.*

Oh and one last thing. Add your personal email to your address. I will try and send you a message every day and perhaps you could do the same to me. Messages of the kind that a mature but infatuated couple might send each other. I suspect your emails are monitored anyway, just because of who you are. Mine will carry just my initial L and will come from inside the email ring-fence the English government maintains. Don't mention anything about Paris or your visit – or what we plan to do when I come over. If there are people reading our emails then let them wonder a bit about who I am; but we need them to conclude that you are taking me away for a couple of days' R&R. What little I know of you, Harry, suggests to me that such outbursts of new romance aren't exactly unknown in your life. So, with luck, these messages will be just taken as evidence of your latest conquest. The one firm thing you need to know – the date when I will get to you, the day before we need to set off for Cornwall, will come on the small device I gave you. That is the only message this machine will send you, so don't forget about it. Now let's get dressed and out of here."

She headed for the bathroom and about 15 minutes later reappeared, wearing of course the clothes she had worn the previous evening. As they got to the door of the room to leave (Harry had had little problem putting his own things together in his modest case), she turned to him and moved close. *"Harry, I don't want you doing anything you don't want to do. If you get back to London and decide to pull out of the Cornwall trip, just make it clear in one of your messages. For example, just say you and I can't meet for a bit. I will understand and I promise I will be able to find another way of doing what I have to do. But if you are willing to go ahead, I also promise you'll have a pleasant few days, even if the scoop turns out to be illusory."* She kissed him again long and hard, opened the door and was gone.

Harry met up with Tara again in the reception area of the hotel, a little before they were supposed to be collected and taken back to the airport. It was Saturday, just 5 days after they had arrived yet Harry felt as though it had been weeks. If he didn't know that he could see Lise again soon,

110

Harry wondered how he would have felt. As it was, he felt so good.

Tara's mood seemed to match his own. She said that Friday had been 'wonderful', a day of sightseeing and shopping. And, when he looked, Harry realised that Tara had added a whole new case to her baggage for the return visit. The driverless car was much less of a threat to Harry this time. They retraced their steps to the military airport, left with as few formalities as they had come and were back in England by 5pm.

23

THE 'RUN IN'

"How you going to keep them down on the farm? Now that they've seen Paree?"

–From a First World War song

Simon was there to meet them and seemed as anxious to know if Harry's visit had gone well as he was to see Tara back. No doubt, Harry thought, Simon had been on tenterhooks while they were away, given how much weight Hetman was placing on this whole venture. And, Harry thought, Simon perhaps might not have minded losing Tara's dominant presence for a few days, especially as she was clearly so buoyed by her time away. Simon quickly spotted the extra case. But Tara lent over to him and just murmured *"Gerald was very kind and let me have some spending money for us. Harry was so busy, he couldn't spend his share."*

Harry did a slight double-take. This was probably the first time he had heard Hetman referred to by his given name; but, as he quickly reflected, Tara was probably on pretty good terms with Hetman, otherwise she would never have been entrusted with her chaperone duties. Harry smiled to himself. On the flight back, Tara had spent at least 15 minutes with Harry rehearsing what she would be saying about how busy Harry had been. If asked, he was to mention how they had actually passed very little time in each other's company because he had been so busy – other than the late night review each day that she had demanded. If you didn't think too much about what Tara might have been doing over those few days, the story had the merit of being true, although not the whole truth.

Harry checked back into his London hotel. The deal with Hetman had been that Harry should use this whenever around so that Hetman could get to see him at short notice if need be. Harry didn't even think about inviting Carol over for the evening; Lise and thoughts of her were all he wanted for company.

A good night's sleep and a lazy Sunday morning with the papers improved Harry's sense of well-being further still. These were the papers carrying the breaking news (hardly news to Harry of course) that the Prime Minister would not be standing again at the forthcoming election, for unspecified 'health reasons'. Harry knew many of those whose by-line came with the story and could guess that Hetman and friends had been preparing the ground for the story for a couple of days. The reviews of the PM's career and achievements in the papers were too full (and fulsome) to have been carved out by a pressured hack who had been given only last-minute news of the story. Harry could imagine that, by midweek, Hetman and friends would have moved the story on, to prepare the ground for 'exciting proposals by a new generation of PDP leaders.' That in turn would no doubt trigger details of Hetman's ideas and then, a day or two later, the articles Harry was supposed to deliver.

Hetman confirmed that broad timetable when he arranged to visit Harry over tea at the hotel that afternoon. Harry felt it was all slightly unreal, as they sat eating excellent scones (a nice change from the many croissants he had had in Paris) in the hotel that afternoon.

As usual, Hetman wasted little time on the preliminaries. He ran through the likely timetable of events, which were much as Harry had supposed. Then, over a second scone each, complete with jam and double cream, Hetman asked Harry direct *"Where are you now with your review? Tara tells me things went well in Paris, that they found plenty for you to do and that you seemed happy enough. But I wouldn't trust Lise and her friends further than I could throw them. And I must admit to being worried that you would be too easily smitten by a comfortable time in Paris, listening to a bunch of people who will no doubt have had a very different agenda of their own. I kept on thinking of a very old soldiers' song about Paris I heard in my childhood – I didn't want it all going to your head. I want you to stay on the same song sheet as me, even if I don't want you to stay on the farm. "*

Harry had known that Hetman would press him about the conclusions he had reached and had prepared his answer quite carefully. *"Well, Minister, in some ways I'm where I was before I left London. You are right that all the major economies seem to be facing the same fact of rising numbers of ageing people. And you're right that medical advances could quite quickly make those pressures greater and add in turn to the pressure on you here to match the extra spending that would no doubt be required. I can now also see that the people I spoke to in Paris don't – anymore than us here – have any real answer for how to improve the lot of the vast numbers of old people. I mean especially those who have no real family, who perhaps have lost a much loved and needed spouse, and who can be said really to be just 'existing', particularly if they are ill.*

*But – and it's a big but – I was introduced to the idea, which I would never have got here in London – that much of this problem may be of our own making. Real income levels could be much higher than they are here now and they could continue to grow; also that technology could help – maybe a lot – with easing the cost and resource pressure of looking after these people. The underlying challenge of 'how to make old age worthwhile for those living through it' is very real. I accept that. But I found myself asking repeatedly why then are we not doing more to boost income and develop our technology? That's quite over and separate from the question I had here, about whether too many of the goodies are just going to a few of the old. It was clear in everything that Lise and her associates said that, elsewhere in the developed world, there is quite a lot available to **all** the elderly, not just to a select few.*"

Hetman drank the rest of his tea with seeming great attention to it. Then he sat back and looked – not in any very friendly fashion, – at Harry. "*I see*" said Hetman. "*I apologise if what follows seems like a politician's favourite trick. But to deal with your concerns, I want to ask a rhetorical question which has several parts and then give you my answers.*

My question is this. Do you not agree that our electorate in this country is extraordinarily conservative when it comes to change of any kind? Twenty years ago they used to say that the French were resistant to change. But every Election here since we left the EU (itself a deeply conservative move in its way) has supported the view that the electorate generally do not want change of any kind, if it can be avoided.

So in much of Europe they have driverless cars and robots in people's homes for all the good it does them. What happened here? Don't you remember the riots – like the old

*Luddites but this time they won – who opposed any idea of change involving the displacement of human labour by robots? Who successfully opposed any fracking for oil and gas? Who eventually voted to stop immigration almost completely, to 'protect' the environment and British 'culture'? Every time they've had a chance –as with the constraints we now have on internet and other content from abroad – to vote, the Electorate here have voted **against** technology, **against** outside risks and **in favour of** 'more of the same'. How do you think I or any sane politician is going to turn that tide to embrace rapid change? And, without that change, you can kiss goodbye to your ideas of rapid income growth and of being able to 'afford' problems like paying for the elderly.*

People here are quite happy with what they've got; or rather, they are not willing to take the risks that would be needed to improve what I believe was once called 'the commonweal'. That's just a fact. Any changes – and even what I'm proposing for Moving On actually is a big change by our standards – need to be dressed up and nuanced or they won't stand a chance. And a politician like me who espoused the ideas you've come up with wouldn't last a year in office."

Harry didn't reply for a long time. He could see Hetman's logic and he couldn't dispute his assessment of recent history. Harry thought of the prolonged opposition about 20 years before, to replacing paper money with plastic and how, after years of campaigning, even that simple move had nearly been reversed. Especially if any change could be construed as enhancing the threat of foreign involvement in local affairs, people here were indeed unbelievably resistant to change. How else, for example, had people been persuaded in the referendum around 2025 to ban all foreign links with the internet or anything like it? That vote, of course, had been taken only months after the cyber-war that had demonstrated- even to the least aware commentator- that the great 'internet of things' could lead to total chaos. Especially if that meant being in the middle of a trial of 'offensive' strength between the Americans, the Chinese and the Russians. Of course, people moaned about some of the resulting restrictions – perhaps most obviously about the rules that made things like his trip to Paris such an unusual event now. But he had to admit he could see the force of Hetman's argument.

Eventually, it was Hetman who broke the silence. *"Let's move on ourselves. While you've been away, I've been thinking about what we could do to set your mind at rest here about whether Moving On is for all or just for some elite. As I explained earlier, I don't have much time before we need you to deliver your side of our bargain, with the articles about the new proposals. But, if you'd like, I can arrange for you to join a group of about 500 people who have agreed to move to somewhere like Newhome and are at the start of that journey. You can mingle with them and experience with them the first couple of days where they prepare for their new life.*

*I think I can promise, however hard you try, you will not be able to argue that this group is an elite; I'm told they come mostly from the East End and from what used to be called the CDE end of society. Again I'm told they are 'shipping out' mainly because the accommodation they can afford here in London looks pretty unappetising compared with a sea-view and all mod-cons down in the West Country. And they have the sense to see that they should move when they're under 70, not 80. In short, what I can assure **you** is that this group represents a typical example of what our new measures are* *designed to elicit from tens of thousands, not just from the occasional 500. Mixing with them may help you write the kind of material that might inspire other people of similar age to follow them!"*

Harry felt he could hardly refuse Hetman's offer of this short trip, though his gut feeling was that it would only be a partial resolution of the concern that had been nagging him since Newhome – that something was 'wrong' with what he had seen there. *"OK, thanks"* Harry eventually said. *"I imagine you want it done soonest. It's Sunday evening now. If you could have me join this group on Tuesday or Wednesday, I'll do it – and I'll be able to get back in good time for the first of the articles you'll be wanting."* With that, Harry reached for the teapot and then a third scone.

24

CHECKING ON HETMAN

"It is always a relief to believe what is pleasant, but it is more important to believe what is true."
–Hillaire Belloc *The Silence of the Sea.*

As usual, Hetman and Simon sprang into action; and by mid-morning Tuesday, Harry was down at what looked like an old army camp, somewhere on the Salisbury plain. He knew from what he had seen that it was west of Stonehenge but not by much. And, although it was still relatively close to London, the air as he stepped out of the car he had been provided with, felt very different from that in London. Even though he was every inch a 'townie', he breathed in deeply.

Monday had been a safely 'down day' for Harry, though actually he had spent several hours responding to the first of the emails that Lise had promised, which had arrived with him on Sunday evening. Her email, he thought on first reading it, had exactly the elements that she had urged upon him. To any outsider, here was a mature woman clearly smitten with him, following up an obvious earlier acquaintance. It was warm, passionate in places, but at the same time carefully avoiding any detail that would link the acquaintanceship to Paris. Rather ungratefully, he had

119

even wondered once whether Lise might have done some similar dissembling before, given how impressive was the end product.

Harry found it very difficult to respond to Lise in like kind. His first effort had looked like that of a love-sick schoolboy. His second effort in contrast reminded him of the kind of memo he had often sent his editor – impersonal and dismissive. It had actually taken him nearly 3 hours of careful drafting to get something that might pass muster. As he had sent it, Harry had mused that, while he was desperate to see Lise again, he hoped that her visit would be soon so that he wouldn't have to concoct too many responses like it.

Otherwise, Harry had settled into a routine of looking for a message on the little machine she had given him – first thing each morning, last thing at night and several times during the day. So far nothing; but what else could he sensibly expect? Harry had arranged with Simon that he could be assured of continued email contact while he was on this short trip into the unknown. He could now do no more that await the dates from Lise and fulfil his current brief mission for Hetman. Harry also sent short messages to his editor and his usual copy-writer cover at the paper. These messages had said that the series of articles that Hetman and the editor were expecting might begin sometime within the next 10 days.

The set up that Harry had joined near Stonehenge had some similarities to Newhome, especially in that he was greeted and shown round by a manager. But this camp was on a much smaller scale than Newhome; and, as the manager Adam West explained, all it did was to take a couple of hundred people at a time and provide a very short-term half-way house from their old life to the location they would be moving on to. Adam, Harry thought, could only be a little younger than Harry himself and he said that about 100 people were due into the camp that afternoon, with more to come in the days after. They would be staying maybe 72 hours, which time would be spent preparing them for their new life.

With a little questioning, Harry established that this preparation had 4 aims. One was to check each individual's medical history and, if necessary, to conduct simple tests and checks at the camp hospital, so that they could be allocated at the other end to a suitable GP. (The people arriving were, Adam said, supposedly relatively young and fit so he foresaw little problem there this time.) A second element was to brief them on the sea-side town they were going to – which basically meant showing them maps of the town and identifying where they were going to be housed. This included providing a virtual walk-through of the town on screen so that they would not arrive completely unprepared. A third element was to explain how the money was handled and handed out; and finally the 4th element was to cover the broad range of possible hobbies and activities (and jobs) that they could explore on arrival.

Harry found Adam disarmingly frank. *"People arrive here"* he said *"fresh from leaving their old haunts. For many of them, this is the first time perhaps that they realise the enormity of the step they've taken. We find that things like a proper medical check-over, which they may never have had, or at least not for years given the state of the NHS back East, really help to boost morale. And we cement that by making sure the food here is great – the Army never ate like this – and by providing lots of free alcohol. We keep them for 3-4 days – it depends a bit on what we find out about them, especially on their health; and on how well organised the town is at the other end. When it's time for them to move on, we send them on in groups of about 35, in a special coach. One or two coaches a day at most, so that the town at the other end isn't swamped with new arrivals."*

"I didn't see any perimeter wall or anything to keep people here. Do you ever get people who back out at this last step?" asked Harry. "A handful of cases I can think of over about 2 years" replied Adam. "We are usually able to identify any likely problem cases pretty quickly, isolate them and really turn the charm offensive on for them. It's amazing how, in most cases, the whole group develops a kind of mass holiday mood which tends to buoy up expectations. That in turn makes any back-sliders feel they'd be letting the side down if they quit now. To be totally honest, I have a personal interest in this working well – I get a bonus based on the number of people I process and send on. But I can assure you that the drop-outs have never been numerous enough to lose me sleep. More fool them I say, if they don't want to go."

25

WATCHING THEM 'MOVE ON'

To change and to improve are 2 different things
–German proverb

The 100 or so new arrivals came in within the hour. The rest of that day and the next then passed quite pleasantly for Harry. Adam had been right. The food was good and the alcohol plentiful. When Harry wasn't drinking gin, his preference was for red wine and that preference was readily indulged here.

Harry had arranged with Adam that he would have the run of the camp; and he chose just to dip in to the various briefings that had been arranged. These briefings – as Harry expected – were resolutely upbeat. But, even so, and thinking back to what he had seen (and been impressed by) in Newhome, Harry could not argue that the picture being given was incorrect in any important way. A couple of times Harry actually chipped in a contribution to a briefing, for example explaining how he had seen the money in Newhome being handed out and used. He hadn't intended to do this; but he quickly realised that, if he spoke up in this way, it would be much easier for him to strike up conversations with individuals during the regular break periods.

And here, when he did this, even Harry had to admit, this group did at least seem to be exactly what Hetman had said – not a Party member in sight. Very ordinary people with a lifetime of what Harry would have regarded as drudgery behind them, now looking forward to a much easier and relaxed life.

When Harry brought the conversation round to what they felt that would be losing by Moving On, he found no obvious themes or concerns. He did detect that a good number of them seemed to be childless or to have only a single child who was now an adult and firmly 'on their own'. One couple – from Hackney who had worked respectively as a cleaner and a motor mechanic through a long working life – admitted that they were moving largely to evade the woman's mother. She was now in her 80s, unwell and totally refused to consider Moving On herself. As the wife put it *"We've already given about 15 years of our lives to looking after her. She'll go on for ever. It was time for Fred and me to think of ourselves."*

Harry also found that Adam had been right in saying that the group was largely upbeat in mood and determined to enjoy everything they were doing. It obviously helped that many of the group knew at least a few of the others – as neighbours or sometimes old local friends. By the Wednesday evening, Harry had concluded that, for this group at least, elitism wasn't an issue; and they were going happily and knowingly on this adventure.

From Tuesday evening on, Harry also had the distraction of responding to another lengthy and romantic email from L. And, in fact, it took him until Wednesday lunchtime to draft a response he thought would do. No sooner had this been sent than the little device Lise had given him pinged once quietly and Harry found himself looking at a short message. This said no more than 'Will be with you by Sunday. Hope you can arrange the sea-air for Monday/Tuesday, the theatre for Tuesday Love L.' That was enough to make it hard for Harry not to seek Adam out and demand to be taken back to London immediately. With a good deal of effort, Harry restrained himself until Wednesday evening. He then told Adam that his visit had been successfully concluded and expressed the hope that he could get out of their way and be shipped back to London soonest.

Adam was almost as pleased to see the back of Harry as Harry was pleased at the prospect of getting back to London. Less than 100 hours until he could see Lise again. He knew that he could readily arrange what was needed to make possible the trip that Lise wanted. Or at least it would be easy, provided Simon was as grateful as he should be that Harry was coming back with only positive things to tell Hetman. After another excellent meal that evening, Harry found himself on a phone provided by Adam, back to Simon, setting out what he – Harry – wanted on his return to London.

26

THE TRIP TO CORNWALL

Two happy days are seldom brothers

–Bulgarian proverb

By 12 the following day, Thursday, Harry was back in Simon's office having asked to be taken there direct. Harry was in a hurry. *"Simon, I'm pleased to say Hetman's plan worked pretty well. I will sit down over the next few days and write those articles he wants. Let's say I can have 5 completed – which he can spread out as he likes – by this time next week. He'll get what he wants. In the meantime though there is something I need you to help with."* Simon replied that, as long as it was nothing unreasonable, he was sure he could help, as he had promised on the phone the night before. And Harry went over exactly what he needed.

"I'm having a couple of days away with a girl. I need to be able to take a car down to Cornwall on Monday, stay at a really nice hotel on the coast there, do the south coast on Tuesday and then get back here Wednesday. I've been pretty busy for you the last few weeks. This is my R&R time and I can assure you the girl is worth the effort. I promise I will have the articles ready for you by next Thursday morning. And I can arrange the hotel and anything else myself. I just

need you to provide a decent car I can drive for a few days – I don't want some prat in uniform driving us around. And I'd like a laissez-passer signed by you that authorises me to travel where I like in that area. I had an embarrassing time a couple of years ago when I got pulled over by the police down in Hampshire. I was given a lot of grief because I had nothing to show that I was on holiday not on a reporting assignment. I don't want something like that – or anything else – upsetting this young lady."

Simon smiled indulgently. *"So the air at Newhome got you in the mood for sharing sea-side breezes with your new womon. Your needs are not unreasonable and I can fix all that within the hour, even though I do think you're a bit old to be having 'romantic' weekends away by the sea. Still, each to his own. I presume you can now check out of your hotel here in London. Even Hetman doesn't have access to unlimited funds and I think you've probably eaten and drunk your way round the hotel menu enough for the time being. And you'll want to get back to familiar ground to start your writing efforts. I must say how pleased I am this has all gone so well. When we're through with the articles, Tara said you must come to dinner – and that would include your lady friend too if you want."*

Simon was as good as his word. Harry went and checked out of the hotel, bringing his small quantity of luggage back with him. By then Simon had the laissez-passer ready, together with a very decent and new hatchback saloon. *"I called in a favour"* said Simon. *"It occurred to me you would want something to impress the young lady; and a normal official car would hardly do the trick. As I implied before, I don't know how you have the energy at your age. But enjoy your trip and I'll see you back here Thursday morning."*

Harry had a parking space near his Victoria flat even though he didn't possess a car; and by early evening he was back in his flat. Simon was right. Harry had had enough by now of hotel living. This was **his** place. A couple of beers, a take-away ordered in; and he was ready to start the first article by 8pm. In an unusually self-disciplined manner, he had decided on the way back from Stonehenge that he would make good and quick inroads to the articles. An hour on Friday morning should take care of the hotel and ordering the theatre tickets. He would then aim to complete the articles by Sunday afternoon at the latest. This timetable had 2 obvious benefits. It would stop him from (or at least make it less likely for him to spend all his time) day-dreaming until she arrived. He had no doubt by the way that she would be there as promised. And, if the articles were done, he could then relax and enjoy every minute with her on this trip that she so wanted to make. With that thought, he reached for his PC and another beer.

27

GETTING THE ARTICLES READY

Harry had already planned how the 5 articles might go. Each needed to be complete on its own and to be readable as an on-going story. To get and keep readers' attention, he would need to have a human interest strap line from the outset. He knew he also needed to avoid appearing to preach to anyone.

Based on that thinking, Harry had very quickly come up with a plausible approach. He would start with the story of 3 people, 2 relatively young, 1 much older (because Harry saw the particular attractions of moving for the genuinely elderly). Why they were looking to move on; what they hoped to get out of it in terms of a better life. Then he would follow that up with his own commentary on how those aspirations might turn out in practice based on what he, Harry, had seen at Newhome. And the last article could resolve into a short personal Q & A that each reader could complete, to establish whether (more likely 'when') that reader should be thinking about moving on in their own case.

Harry had already decided that the flavour he would

leave in these 5 articles would be a strongly positive one. Moving On **was** attractive, especially but not solely for the more elderly. It would only become more so as the programme built up. The central theme would be about how people could get their own lives back and enjoy a more pleasant and focused retirement, which would offset any initial concerns about leaving family and friends behind.

He had no qualms about making up the case studies – they wouldn't be people he had met in the last few weeks but the stories would of course draw from all those he had heard. Journalistic licence of a very limited kind. He was also fairly sure that he could paint a picture that was positive without seeming to read more like PR. This was where his existing credibility with readers would be critical. And he was also sure that he could tell a story which *did* cover the downsides of Moving On, without destroying the overall optimistic message.

One other thing Harry decided early on was that his articles needed to carry the absolute minimum of facts about the ageing population and the costs of just accepting more of the same rather than of something like Moving On. He had to focus on the human interest implications. On reflection, he thought Hetman – and Harry's editor – couldn't object to his pieces being accompanied by a couple of thoughtful factual background articles that would set out the wider context and bathe people in the statistics that he, Harry, had found so persuasive. That meant his 5 articles would require him to complete 7 altogether; but he wasn't going to have someone else put those facts together, especially not as Harry now felt he was as well qualified as anyone to write them.

One thing Harry had forecast accurately. The booking at the hotel down near Rock (he had identified somewhere suitable as soon as he had got back from Paris) and the tickets for The Minack took less than an hour to obtain on Friday morning. He discovered that the show at The Minack would be the last of the season – an amateur production of a Gilbert & Sullivan at that. Harry made a mental note to pack some warm clothing and maybe wet weather gear as well. Cornwall at the end of September, although they had had an Indian summer from which he had benefitted on his trip to Newhome, could be pretty cold and unwelcoming he imagined. With that thought, he returned to the articles.

By Sunday afternoon, all 5 and the 2 background pieces were written to a standard that Harry thought he could finish off quickly, according to anything that Hetman particularly wanted. Harry felt relaxed about making minor changes of presentation if Hetman asked. He drew the line at any attempt at editorial influence; and, to be fair to Hetman, the man had never tried that. Harry would also be happy if John and Claire were allowed to review the background articles; after all, most of the statistics he wanted to use had been provided by those 2.

The only break Harry had allowed himself was to go and pick up a couple of bottles of decent wine, 2 good fillet steaks and a few prepared vegetables that he could easily microwave. Harry had no illusions about his capacity to cook. But also he wanted every minute alone he could get with Lise and so had no intention of wasting time on Sunday night going out to eat. Harry topped the menu off with a selection of cheese and breads, knowing full well – from what he had seen in Paris – that London shops couldn't compete with what had been on offer in France. But it would be good enough – and that had always been his motto in such things.

Time went by and Sunday afternoon became Sunday evening. Harry began to get a little worried. But just as the tension was starting to hurt, the outside doorbell of his bloc of flats rang and Lise identified herself when he answered. *"Thank God* "said Harry *"I'm on the second floor."*

The inside bell for the flat itself went about a minute later. He opened it and there she was, looking a little flustered or fraught he thought but as beautiful as she had been in Paris. Lise stepped inside, quickly embraced him but, as quickly, moved away. *"Well"* she said *"I've made it. It was just as well you are so close to the centre of London. My meetings went on until about 6 pm and then it was time to check out of the hotel and get to you without – I hope – anyone being able to follow me."* "You're making this sound more and more like something out of a spy novel." replied Harry. *"Why would anyone want to follow you? Look, I've got good steak and wine. Let me cook quickly and then we can sit down and you can tell me a bit more about what is going on."*

Harry was as good as his word and within 20 minutes the steaks and a selection of vegetables were on a plate, together with a large glass of red wine for each of them. He knew better than to try and intersperse his culinary efforts with any serious talk, so their conversation in those 20 minutes was limited. Lise spent the time moving round the sitting room and kitchen of his flat, picking up the odd photo or piece of art and asking Harry about it.

They sat down at Harry's small table. He raised his glass to her and said *"I can't tell you how good it is to see you or how much I've been missing you, silly though that may sound. Everything you asked for has been arranged and I have a great car waiting 5 minutes away for me to drive you out of London tomorrow. So, if you can, tell me more about what we are up to down in Cornwall. Otherwise tell me how glad you are to see me – if you are – and what our next few days may hold."*

"I'd rather not say more about what we are going to be doing until we are safely down in Cornwall" Lise said. "I promise I will then. In the meantime, just trust me and relax. I like good company and I think that is exactly what you could be – seriously good company. Oh, and let's get one thing out in the open from the beginning. I'm sure you're hoping that I'll be a bit more 'forthcoming' than when we shared a bed in Paris. I will, Harry, I will. But not until we've accomplished what I have to do, which will be Tuesday night or never. Until then, I feel taut like a stretched string. I'd be no good company for you; in fact if we tried before I can forget about all this, I think it would greatly damage the chances of our ending up really close to each other, which is what I take it you want. So, to compensate for being standoffish now, I've arranged that I can spend the whole of this week with you, if you want me. And I do promise that I won't keep you at a distance then!"

Harry had decided days ago that he would play it long and relaxed with Lise. He really was in for the long haul and in his heart he knew that it was either this girl or probably a continuing life on his own. For ever. The second option just wasn't something that he could contemplate.

So the evening passed in what to Harry at least seemed like an unsettling but not wholly bad dream sequence. Lise asked him about his family, his background and interests all the way through the meal. And he did his best to establish some facts about her, though he would have had to admit that she found out 4 times as much about him as he did of her background and interests. Lise occupied his bed while he slept on the sofa in the living room. And by the time they were ready to leave in the morning, Harry felt that **he** was the one wound up like a stretched string – and one that would break if things continued as they were.

28

BETWEEN ROCK...

Happiness is not a horse; you cannot harness it.
–Russian proverb

Harry's mood lightened as they drove out of London. The car moved like a dream. The weather was sunny and pleasant in the best autumnal spirit. And once he had got out of London on the M4 there was – as he had expected – very little traffic to contend with. They stopped at a pub near Taunton to enjoy what Harry was able to describe as 'traditional English pub food'. Lise seemed to enjoy it, if not the half-pint of Guinness he offered her. And her attitude to him also seemed to relax the further away from London that they got.

The roads weren't as well maintained as they had been in his youth. But this was more than compensated for by the lack of traffic. And no sign anywhere of police or other interference. When 2 lanes went down to 1, as they entered Cornwall, he was still able to drive at 50 or better. 5 hours of driving plus the hour or so for lunch deposited them at the discreet and high-quality hotel near Rock that he had booked into.

That evening, after a quiet but – to him- enjoyable walk along the rather jagged seashore there, the pattern of the previous evening was repeated. Though this time the meal took place in a pleasant and largely empty dining room at the hotel, rather than in Harry's living room. Lise then made herself at home on her side of the bed, obviously reckoning – correctly – that Harry could and would keep his natural instincts under curb for another 24 hours.

The next day was spent quietly. A good English breakfast – which Lise claimed to like more than her native croissants – was followed by another, longer walk on the shore. At one point Lise insisted on stopping to search for cowrie shells but was unsuccessful. As Harry had no idea even what a cowrie looked like, he was forced to stand to one side and content himself with trying to skip stones across a relatively flat sea. He could see some parallel between this time-filling activity and these 2 days so far with Lise.

Over a brief lunch, Lise did say to him that they needed to leave Rock before 4, as the drive to The Minack was quite a long one. *"I believe it's a very impressive place, Harry. An open-air theatre carved out of rock with a dramatic sea-view background. I think we're going to see 'The Pirates of Penance' and the girl who told me about the theatre said that the pirates in the cast often swarm up the steep back of the theatre on ropes to make a dramatic entry. Sounds fun. Anyway, let's see."*

Once they were in the car and heading down the main (only) road to the southern coast where The Minack lay, Harry felt the time had come when he had to know more. *"OK, LIse, I've been very restrained in what I've asked since Sunday evening. But look; it's time to tell me what is really going on and also why everything will be so much better after tonight. Or are you going to have some other reason to keep me at arms' length? I've mentally allocated this*

136

week to winning your heart for life. I'm serious about this. But frankly it's not easy to be serious when we're sleeping in different beds and our conversations resemble one that might be taking place between a relatively distant brother and sister."

29

...AND A HARD PLACE

Man is born unto trouble, as the sparks fly upward.
–Book of Job Chapter 5 Verse 7

Lise turned in her seat and looked at him. "*Poor Harry. I promise you'll feel better about life by this time tomorrow, though whether you will ever end up with my 'heart and love' only time will tell. What I can tell you now is that we must head for a pub, The Good Shepherd, which is near The Minack. I can give you directions when we get to the final part of the journey.*

We are going to eat there before the performance and there we will be joined by a man I have never met before. He is a US GI and, officially, is on shore leave, which he happens to be spending in Cornwall doing slightly screwy things like visit an open-air theatre. Anyway, he will turn up at the pub. He knows what I look like and I've seen photos of him. He will join us and then..." she paused, as though thinking how much she should say "*He is based on one of your Scilly Isles which we think has* actually *been rented by the US military from the UK Government. There, we think, the US is running some kind of containment camp where they keep Muslim extremists and anyone else they don't like the look of, out of what they see as harm's– i.e. the public's*

138

– way. 25 years ago, it was at a place called Guantanamo. They shut that and claimed it hadn't been replaced. But we think it has – here in England."

Whatever Harry had expected Lise to say, it wasn't this. Questions and objections tumbled through his thoughts and he blurted them out in a short and not necessarily coherent stream. *"Who in God's name do you work for?"* he asked. *"How can you possibly know what this man has access to? How do you know that what he tells you is true? How can he and you prove it? What have I got involved with?"*

Lise waited until she was fairly sure there would be no further outburst from Harry. *"Well, Harry. The first thing I need to admit to you is that, just like you, I am a journalist by trade. I work freelance but tend to get published in the upmarket US rags. Not under the name 'Lise' I should add. Over my time in Europe, I have come to know some good people who are concerned about the state of the world. So I can promise you I'm working on the side of the good guys not for the CIA or some other agency. When I offered you the scoop of a lifetime, what I really meant was that you could be left to do what you will, in England, about the story, while I write up the American side of things. If events turn out as I expect, there are likely to be lots more people coming forward with 'news' about this camp and lots of avenues I will be able to explore. For England, I don't know how you'll want to play it. But I couldn't believe my luck when I discovered that you were coming to Paris. I've checked up that, insofar as there are still straight journalists in England who publish the truth and be damned, you are one of the best. Hence my offer.*

We – my friends and I – got involved with you a bit by chance. When the English Government approached their French counterparts about a month ago, the French just didn't know what to do. We heard about it through our grapevine; and the French were only too pleased to hand it all over to us, to organise a week for you covering ageing and medicine in the EU and in the US. Like you, I had to immerse myself in a lot of facts and figures. But like you I'm a quick learner and several of the people I brought in to talk to you really are experts in that field. They just also happen to be among the good guys.

Perhaps it's also obvious now why I asked for your help. With you as 'cover', I could hope to get down to Cornwall and meet my contact without anyone in London being any the wiser. If you hadn't come along, I'd have found another way. Instead, it's working like a dream – **except** that I found you to be a really nice guy and someone who, yes, I could perhaps fall for in a big way. There has been no-one significant in my life for several years now; and as I promised you'll get your chance, a real chance in the next few days.

Of course there are some risks. But among the good guys there are only 2 of us who know the identity of this possible informant, the girl in The Scillies who first made friends with him and now me. His life and liberty will indeed be under threat once he has spoken out. But we've promised to give him 4 or 5 days start to 'disappear' (and for me to get safely back to France after I've been with you) before we run any articles; and I'm carrying enough money to help him do just that.

As for evidence, the deal is that he has to have photographs and background material – like the names of some of the inmates – that will be used when I break the story. This information will have that 'edge of truth' that most people look for when they read something like this. As I say, I expect – after a volley of official denials – that *more informants will quickly appear; and then we're away. I don't yet know anything about the English side of this – in particular who has authorised this and what money must be changing hands. They're things you can follow up if you want; I shall have enough on my plate."*

Harry absorbed this as best he could. Lise had landed him right in the muck. Even if things went as she obviously planned and they could break the story, he would become totally persona non grata in England, while she would never be able to travel to England again. Harry was also of a somewhat cynical turn of mind. What if this American informer was actually a 'plant'? What if the man was faking the supposed evidence and just planned to vanish with the cash? There were just too many 'what ifs' for him to compute.

Unfortunately, he reflected, Lise had timed things all too well. Short of stopping the car and refusing to go on, there was now little he could do and that would certainly wreck any chance he might have with her. She had told him so late that they now barely had time to get to The Good Shepherd. Harry didn't know what to make of Lise's 'confessions' of what she had kept back from him. His first reaction – and that was the one he typically went with when he really didn't know what to do – was that the story was maybe an hour away from emerging or not. Harry could listen to the informant, maybe assess the supposed evidence and then decide whether he wanted to walk away, either from the story or from Lise or both. He still felt the same about her as before and his heart had leapt when she had admitted that she had feelings for him. Surely this plan of action didn't involve too much danger for him or her? Surely it would buy him some time to think?

As she had said, Lise had clear directions to the pub

and they pulled up about 10 to 6. Their table was booked for 6 and the waitress led them into a dining room that was completely empty. When Harry remarked on this, the waitress laughed and said *"Come back at 8 and you'll find a fair few people here. We don't get much call for food this early."*

Lise and Harry sat down at a table for 4 and ordered – a simple starter each and then a main course, steak for him and a Caesar salad for her. The clock ticked round, past 6 and then got to 6.15. *"Are you sure he's coming?"* Harry said in a quite unnecessary whisper (seeing that there was still no-one else in the room). But before Lise could answer, the dining room door opened and a man of about 30 walked in. He was of medium height and with the kind of build and muscle tone that said military or police.

The man looked round to confirm that Lise and Harry were the only diners; and then he looked harder at Lise. He came over to them. *"May I join you?"* he said with an obvious accent that said to anyone who knew their Americans that he was from the South, probably Georgia or thereabouts. Lise responded. *"Of course, make yourself at home. We are having an early supper and are on the way to The Minack . Maybe you're going that way too? If so, we could certainly give you a lift – always happy to help a fellow American, which is what I am even if I don't sound it."*

The man sat down opposite Lise. *"I was told you'd be on your own. Who's this?"* he tossed his head at Harry as he spoke. Lise saved Harry the problem of replying. *"He's a late addition to the party but believe me he's worth having along. Now you look very much like the photo I was given – Guy Mannering am I right? I hope I look reasonably like the girl you were shown a photo of?"*

"Sure" the man replied *"even prettier".* But let's get down to the business *before the waitress comes in to take my*

order. I don't want to be round here for long; I'm certainly not coming on your theatre trip. If you're the genuine article, I want to see the cash you guys promised. For my part I've put down on paper all I know about the Camp, with the kind of photos and detainee list that you asked for. Plenty of evidence for whatever you have planned. Here it is" he dragged an A5-sized envelope out of his pocket. *"I can't expect you to hand over the cash before you've had a look at the contents; I hope you're quick readers. Just show me the cash – 25,000$ we agreed- and I'll show you the documents. You read them, tell me OK; I let you keep the docs, you hand over the cash and I'm out of here."*

30

TRUTH WILL OUT

"No-one speaks the truth when there's something they must have."

–Elizabeth Bowen *The House in Paris*

At this point, the waitress came in with Lise's and Harry's main dishes and laid them in front of the couple. She then turned to the American and said *"And what can I get you, sir?"* *"I don't feel hungry"* he replied *"maybe I'll eat later. Just bring me a large whisky and water please. That's one of the few English customs I've taken a liking to."* *"Of course"* the girl replied and moved back and out through the door, shutting it behind her.

Lise looked angry. *"This wasn't the deal. You were going to answer questions that I could use for my paper. I want to understand, get a proper feel for, the place you are working at. Not just look at some paper portfolio you've put together."* *"Well, this is how it's going to be."* Mannering replied. *" Just look at what's in the envelope. There is more there than I could tell you in a week; and, while I suppose someone could argue the photos are rigged, there's real explosive stuff in there, like the top 10 detainees who are kept in solitary confinement. It'll blow your socks off. All I get is 25 lousy thousand that I'm probably going to use up in a month hiding from the guys who'll be after me once this becomes public. Oh and by the way, you must stick with the 5 days from now start you promised before your first piece. I'm on shore leave; and I've enough friends to help me disappear from their view. But if I were unlucky enough to be caught, don't think for a moment that I wouldn't spill every bean I could to get myself a better deal. That girl of yours in St. Mary's, your role, the money and now this English guy too. They'd find him pretty damn quick if they know where to look."*

Harry couldn't think of anything to say. To have something to do (and because it smelled good) he cut and ate a couple of mouthfuls of steak. Lise, in contrast, pushed her plate away, seized the envelope, tore it open and began riffling through the contents.

About 3 minutes later, the waitress appeared with the man's whisky and then made herself scarce. There was an atmosphere in the room that even she, without knowing any of what was actually happening, could have sensed from 20 yards. Lise grunted once or twice as she turned the pages. Several of the photos seemed to interest her particularly, as did a list which Harry assumed was that of the main residents. After no more than 5 minutes, she looked up, actually smiled at Guy, and said – reaching for the bag she always kept with her – *"We'll I guess you have fulfilled the substance of the deal even if not to the exact letter. Here's the cash; you can count it if you want but it's all there in bundles of 1,000 made up for us by the bank."*

She reached into her bag, pulled out a sizeable envelope of her own and passed it to Guy, who tore it open with the same intensity that Lise had used on his envelope. The 3 of them looked at each other.

That, Harry thought afterwards, was how 3 armed

men got into the room, through the main dining room door, before anything registered with Harry that there was something wrong.

Harry had never had a gun pointed at him before, let alone what looked very like a snub-nose machine gun of the kind he associated with Hollywood thrillers. One of the men called *"All secure"* and then a fourth person entered the room, one Gerald Hetman.

Harry had also never had his world collapse on him in an instant like a burst balloon; but that too he experienced in the next 5 seconds. For a minute no-one spoke. Lise sat there with the envelope in her hand, Guy with her envelope in his and Harry, incongruously, with his fork and knife in his hands. Time seemed to be in suspense and then Hetman spoke. *"Time I think to restore a little order."* He leant over and took the envelope from Lise's unprotesting hand; and then – with more difficulty – detached Guy's hands from the envelope he was holding. He said to Harry *"You can you eat a bit more of that excellent-looking steak before we adjourn to somewhere more convenient for us."*

Guy rose to his feet but quickly subsided back into the chair as one of the snub-nosed machine guns came ominously close to his midriff. Eventually, Lise broke the silence. *"How did you know? How did you find us?"*

Hetman smiled indulgently at her. *"How could we not know? You've left an elephant-sized trail even before you joined up with Harry; and since he's been on board, the trail could have been made by 2 elephants. One of your colleagues in Paris, Lise, has kept us in the loop for months. If you successfully ever get back to Paris, you'll find out who that was, because he won't be there any longer. And Harry, did you really think we wouldn't be monitoring your every move and message? Did you really think that a couple of Dear Harry~ emails signed 'L' would fool us for a moment?*

146

Did you never think that the car Simon so kindly provided for you might not have a GPS-finder attached to it?

The only things we weren't sure of were who the turncoat was in the American ranks. So we needed to let you all meet up. By the way, the Americans will be very grateful for his return; perhaps they'll put him in with the other extremists in the Camp on The Scillies. And we also wanted to make sure we had a full idea of what information he had obtained – so, many thanks Mr. Mannering for the envelope.

I think now it's time to let the pub get back to business. I must go and thank the manager for his help to the Crown. And it's time for you 3" – he indicated Lise, Harry and Guy – *"to go your separate ways. Or perhaps I should say the different ways we have arranged for you. There are 3 cars waiting outside, each to transport one of you to the first destination we have planned for you."*

Lise was the first to be pulled to her feet and escorted out of the room. Harry hadn't looked at her before, as though pretending that none of this was happening and that this could be achieved by looking down at the table. Lise grimaced at him. *"I'm so sorry, Harry. I shall always think of you."* And then she was gone.

31

NO WAY OUT?

Deos fortioribus adesse (The gods are on the side of the stronger)

–Tacitus Histories Book 4, Chapter 17

Harry had been in confinement 4 or 5 days now; he wasn't sure exactly how long. The drive from the pub to here had only been 30 minutes or so; but time doesn't mean much when you have your head in a black hood/bag and your hands cuffed behind you. The men with him on the journey had provided no commentary.

Each day so far had been the same. Food and drink brought 3 times a day by guards who said nothing even when he shouted at them. No threats; no questioning, no human communication at all – which he found oddly disturbing. Harry spent his time alternating between 2 states of mind. First, and most often, thoughts of Lise and fears for her safety; he had never really got to know any of the others on the team back in France, nor did he really care about them so it was always just Lise in his mind. Was she dead already? If so, when – which he longed to do –would he join her? Second, and in some ways more painful to him, reflections on just how inadequate their preparations had been, how laughable the 2 of them must have seemed to Hetman and his professionals. He and Lise had never had a chance. How could he ever have thought that they did?

What Harry didn't question during this enforced pause for thought was why had he agreed so readily to do what Lise had wanted. Even when – in Rock – it had become apparent that she had at least one other persona, and that he actually knew very little about her. He didn't care. Whatever happened to him, he decided he would cling to the thought that it would have been worth it.

The next morning, a different guard appeared and actually spoke to Harry unbidden. *"Gather your things. I'll come back for you in 10 minutes."* It took Harry perhaps 30 seconds to pull his sad little pile of possessions together into the rucksack which had been pulled from his car outside the pub and thrown in with him. In due course, the guard returned, alone, and led Harry down the passage outside. Down stairs and into the courtyard where one of the grander official cars sat waiting, engine running. Harry's rucksack was tossed into the boot and the near-side rear door then held open for him by the guard. The heavily tinted glass meant that, only as Harry bent his head to enter, did he realise that there was someone already sitting in the back seat – Hetman!

Hetman looked pleased with himself and with the world, smiling gracefully as Harry settled in without a word. *"Make yourself comfortable, Harry"* he said as the car moved off.

"What have you done with her, you bastard?" Harry eventually managed to say in what must have seemed like a stage whisper. *"Now, Harry. No need for melodramatics. I have merely come down to put your mind at rest about the girl you call Lise and then to explain exactly how we*

intend to move on, avoiding any further waves in the process.

First, your friend. Lise is safe and already back in our Paris embassy. She will be released just as soon you are on your way. I have a few photos with me so that you can see for yourself that she looks well, as no doubt you might have trouble taking my word for it. But I do hope you can see that it has been, for me, a positive godsend to have this little group of international do-gooders dropped in our lap in such compromising circumstances. And, from that, you should be able to work out that I, of all people, could never pass such an opportunity by – even if it mean letting your little friend scuttle home. Our informant in her group – it was Jochen by the way – is a different matter. He has proved himself admirably in recent months. You can be sure I will have further work for him in good time; and he is already out of Paris.

So, what have we managed in the last 5 days? Well first and foremost a Treaty of Mutual Respect – wonderful title, my own idea – initialled with France. It is designed to make sure your little escapade doesn't get repeated with any foreign sovereign help any time soon. How fortunate that France see the need to look after their nationals so well and to avoid getting on the wrong side of the Americans. And how fortunate that Americans will pay so handsomely to maintain illusions – in this case that things like Guantanimo Bay were long past and gone, not recreated here. They already pay handsomely to 'rent' one of the larger Scilly Isles from us – as well as the other facilities they have here. And, of course, they have just as great a desire as we do for these things to stay under wraps. The only thing they immediately have to do is to tighten up shore leave for their nationals working in the Camp – not a great hardship for anyone, I should think.

For her part, Lise will know – if she has listened to what she has been told – that any further moves on her part to stir up trouble will be dealt with swiftly and severely. And I hope that the ease with which Jochen worked his way into her circle will serve as adequate reminder to her that it's best to keep her 'do-gooding' to demonstrations and harmless rantings in her press. I doubt, though, whether she will even feel like doing that now, given the fright she has had.

We can't say anything about all this in public, of course. But I can assure you that those who need to know within the PDP are already aware. And that can only stand me in very good stead now that our beloved Leader has announced that he is stepping down on health grounds. I think all this couldn't have played out better.

I've thought for a long time that someone like Lise would come along to try what she did. In one way, your involvement was an unnecessary complication. But, thanks to you, I could – as it were – and purely metaphorically – kill 2 birds with 1 stone. Ever since I got you involved with Moving On, I had a slight unease about how – if necessary – we might keep you biddable in the months and years to come. Now, you've answered my unease."

"So, what exactly will happen to me?" asked Harry. He cared little for himself if Lise was indeed safe; having to trust Hetman on that was unpalatable but Harry could see how his logic had run. Even Hetman surely could not go round eliminating foreign nationals. But he had to ask about his own future.

"Well, Harry, I'm afraid we can't have you back with us in London for obvious reasons. It seems only fitting – in the light of the glowing articles you will be writing about Moving On – that, since we plan to reduce the minimum age to 60, you should be the very first citizen to take that offer up. Even though you are well below the new age limit. With immediate effect, of course.

When people read your articles, it won't be a surprise to

them when you close the last one with the announcement that you have been the first person taking up the new offer; and that you have chosen to seize the day, and not to return, even for a farewell party. No doubt Carol – was it? – and your journalist colleagues will regret that last bit. I'm sure they will drink your health one evening and share a few stories about you. But, as someone once said 'the caravan moves on'; and I suspect you will be largely forgotten within weeks."

"And what if I don't agree, don't go along with your plans? Harry asked. *"Well"* replied Hetman *"it won't make much odds though, of course, it might make Lise's last step back to Parisian life rather 'more difficult'. I've already had your articles drafted out – so they'll come out as we need. Thanks by the way for all the drafting effort you put in last weekend. It means they will genuinely look like you wrote them, because you did write about 80% of them. I think we should stop short of writing about the joys of women like Ingrid in the process, though even here, I'm happy to say your 'efforts' have been beneficial. When you met up with her, she was serving a sentence for repeated prostitution. I offered her an immediate pardon, if she slept with you – in the process providing useful ammunition in case you should ever be difficult. By the way, the film Giorgi took that night was well worth watching; I watched it twice!*

Lastly, if you don't co-operate, it won't make any difference to where you end up and there wouldn't be a last note from you delivered by me to Lise. And I suppose the electronic surveillance we shall have to ask you to accept once you've moved on will have to be a little more intrusive, shall we say. But same outcome, whether you co-operate or not; you will have left the rat-race.

Now, let me show you those pictures I promised you of

Lise back on French ground, albeit not yet quite free of our attentions. I trust you will note the obvious French backdrop and the papers clearly showing that the photos were taken just yesterday. You really wouldn't be worth the bother of my faking such photos. But perhaps you realise that by now. I think we have about an hour before they pick you up– plenty of time to write to Lise if you want."

32

A LAST LETTER

If there's a single lesson that life teaches us, it's that wishing doesn't make it so.

–Lev Grossmans *The Magicians*

My darling Lise.

This is the first and the last real message I shall ever write to you. And how I would have wished for different surroundings in which to write. Instead, I am scribbling this in the back of the car of our Nemesis. And I have to rely on his promise, an unhappy reliance, that this will get to you – and that you will be a free woman when you receive it.

I want to tell you just one thing and ask you 2 favours. The thing to tell you, the only thing in my mind, is how much I love you and shall always love you while there is breath in my body. In truth, I had hardly got to know you; that much was obvious in the bombshells you dropped in the car from Rock. But none of that changes my feelings. Much of my thoughts now are about things we would have done, places we would have gone, had circumstances been kinder. I can't think about the little we did do together, that is too painful. But please take my love as fact, one of the pillars of the universe on which you can rely; I just hope that finds at least an echo within your own heart.

Now, the 2 things I ask. The first is that you forget the cause that brought you and me together; or at least that you do nothing from now on to risk the wrath of the British Government or anyone else. Without evidence, you cannot proceed.

You said once that I didn't know much about you. How right that was. But what little I have now learned makes no difference to me. I may be over 50 and much too old for such flights of fantasy. But you are the first real love of my life; and whether you actually feel anything for me or not I shall always love you.

Now please look ahead. Your life now needs now to look forward not back; that's the second favour I ask. Someone **will** eventually uncover what you were seeking to reveal. As for me, the old of Britain can fare well enough by themselves, without my further involvement. According to our Nemesis I shall get to know a lot of them pretty well though, given what I now know about our Government's activities around England. Who is to say – certainly not me – that their plans for the elderly are not well-meant. What matters for me, though, is simply that you stay safe and well.

Last, something simple and selfish – once in a while think of me, perhaps pull out and re-read this letter, which is all I can say given who will be vetting it. I stress that I have no regrets about what has happened – at least if by that you mean would I wind the clock back a few weeks? If winding the clock back meant never meeting you and living the rest of my life in the meaningless comfort I then enjoyed, then the answer is 'absolutely no'; I am glad that what has happened to me has happened, if that was the only way I was going to meet you.

Live long, live positive, live life to the full my darling –
for both our sakes. You must stay free and safe.
Your love, ever
Harry.

33

MOVING ON

And some there be, which have no memorial...and are become as though they had never been born
—Ecclesiasticus Chapter 44, verse 94

Hetman took the finished note from Harry and put it away in his jacket pocket. *"I assume you're happy to leave me to finish drafting your pieces for the paper? No time really to do anything else. Oh, and by the way, I know all about the little code you have with your editor to prove that anything he gets has actually been written by you. I'm afraid he will undoubtedly conclude that you have written these pieces. Another example of your almost unbelievable naivety."*

The car now drew up at what Harry saw immediately was a cross roads, on one corner of which was a rather sad-looking bus stop, sitting in the middle of what seemed like nowhere. There was also what looked like a petrol pump, by the side of the road. *"We've arranged that the next coach of movers picks you up here. I've ensured that you will at least start out by the sea and somewhere with not too many ancients for company. My driver will now put a small ankle bracelet on you, to make sure that you'll be here when the coach comes – or at least that we can find you quickly if not. Good luck, Harry. Good-bye and – although this may sound odd – thank you."*

The driver's work on the bracelet was soon done and, as the car moved away, Harry stood somewhat disconsolately by the road sign, his rucksack – the sum total now of his worldly possessions – at his feet. The sky was overcast, with a hint of rain in the air; but mercifully no actual rain. It was cold but not bitterly so.

Harry saw behind him some deep trenches, straight lines of perhaps 30 yards in length. And behind them a small stack of large yellow piping of the kind that he associated with water mains, together with a yellow digger, that clashed subtly with the piping. What they were doing in this god-forsaken place he could not imagine. But he also couldn't care.

Breaking into his thoughts came the sound of a coach driving slowly up the road behind him. He turned. At least the coach looked fairly modern though he guessed that the journey he was about to take couldn't last more than an hour or two in all; so it hardly mattered. The coach pulled to a halt by the petrol pump, incongruously seeming to take care to stop exactly by it, as though space round here was at a premium.

The driver, a burly and rather uncouth man of perhaps 40, opened the door and said *"Mr. Woods, if my notes are right. Climb on board and join the sing-along going on here. I've just got to stop and take on some petrol. Then we'll be off."*

He and 2 other men, who were obviously guards but in no uniform, clambered down from the bus. Harry went up the stairs, to be greeted by a raucous welcome from within *"Here's another sea-side punter. Come on mate, don't hold us up. We can't wait to get there. Oh, and have a beer."* This last offer was made by a peroxide blonde of a certain age and girth. Someone who Harry now realised he had met before, just last week among the group of new recruits to Moving On.

Behind her, a fairly full coach of happy and seemingly normal people, mostly he thought in their early 60s. 'Normal people'. Harry mentally breathed a sigh of relief – he couldn't see himself fitting in with old PDP members after what Hetman had done to him. He smiled at the woman. "*Fancy our meeting again out here. I thought you all were supposed to have travelled a few days ago.*" A man, seated near the front, whom Harry also vaguely recognised, waved an open can of beer in the air. "*Delays like always, mate. But at least they've left us beer all the way through.*"

The door shut with a metallic click. Had Harry been looking out of the right window, he would have seen the 3 men in charge of the coach manhandling a pipe across to it and plugging it in to where a petrol lead might reasonably go. Had Harry thought about it, he would have noticed that all the windows of the coach were shut – perhaps not too odd in light of the weather. But it was only about 45 seconds later that Harry, and the rest of the passengers, found that both the door and the windows were sealed shut.

The gas came in with a rush. There was a perhaps 10 second hiatus as people looked at each other and realised that this was not as it should be. Another 10 seconds and half the people at the back of the coach launched themselves into the gangway to get out; while Harry and the peroxide blonde, because they were nearest, wrestled with the door in an unsuccessful effort to open it. Harry looked wildly around. Nothing he could see to smash a window or save himself. The last 2 thoughts Harry had were just that –'nothing I can do' and 'so this is how they are going to do it'.

Had Harry been around to observe the process, he would have seen that it took less than an hour for the gas to disperse, and for the 3 men to move the bodies out of the coach, strip them of valuables, and dump them in to the nearest of the trenches. Maybe another 20 minutes for one of them to use an idle digger conveniently placed there to back fill the trench and hide any obvious trace of what had happened. Another hour or so to eliminate any evidence within the coach of anything untoward. No blood, very little human detritus – gas was obviously an effective way to manage things.

Had Harry been there to ask how often this happened, he might have been told by the men in charge 'about 3 times a week'. Put another way, as Hetman would no doubt have done, 100 people a week, 5,000 a year – moving on in the most efficient cost-saving way possible. Had Harry been there, he might by now also have realised that this might not be the only convenient staging post for Moving On. And at last an explanation for why no Party members in this group – their travel to the West undoubtedly ran further and smoother.

Hetman could be – and no doubt was – proud of his men. And, like much of what Hetman did, the operation could quickly be ramped up if it worked well. No reason why future plans could not quickly run to many thousands of 'normal' people a week, if Harry's articles had their desired effect.